Greener Grass

Lisa D.A. Roberto

First Edition

Fulton Books
Meadville, PA

Published by Fulton Books 2024

ISBN 979-8-89221-159-8 (paperback)
ISBN 979-8-89221-160-4 (digital)

Printed in the United States of America

As I packed the last of my things into the car, I looked back at the house that I was leaving. The house that we raised our children in. The house that we bought and fixed up together. The house that my family was still living in. Was I doing the right thing? What was I thinking? Maybe I could just change my mind and stop this craziness. Or could I?

This was a long time coming. We had not been happy in so long that I didn't even remember what happiness looked like. I kept trying to convince myself that if I could just go and make the first step to get away, I could have everything that I have ever wanted. It had taken me years to take that first step. It was so hard, not because I was afraid of him, but because I was afraid of everyone. What would people think? What would they say? That had always been my biggest fear, the opinions of everyone else. I swore I lived my life for everyone but me. Well, I had finally taken the step toward living for me!

I packed that last of my personal items into my car. I could come back for the rest. Or maybe I would just buy more. I could do whatever I wanted now because I didn't have to answer to anyone.

As I was pulling out of the driveway, I looked back. The pang of pain that no one was watching, running after me begging me not to go. No one was crying or asking me to take them with me. I couldn't help to be disappointed and feel sick that I dedicated my entire life to taking care of everyone else and no one even cared that I was leaving.

I drove through town one last time, passing all the places that we went as a family, the playgrounds, the school, the church, even the little general store. Was I ever going to be able to come back here and have it feel the same? Did I want it to?

I watched our children grow. We worked so hard to make them good people and to be a good family. It was hard work, and we worked hard to provide a better life for them than we had growing up. But somewhere along the line, we lost us. We forgot that we, as a couple, were the foundation of the family. It was all lost in piano lessons, sports, practices, homework, plays, and every event that we had to attend for our respective careers. As an attorney, I was expected to meet with clients and attend outings as needed. The same went for Mark. He was an engineer and was required to attend meetings after hours for proposals for new projects or to consult on current projects. We saw the people that we worked with and for more than we saw each other.

Now, with the children grown and in and out from college, I just could not play the game any longer. I wanted it to work. Believe me, I wanted nothing more than to be married forever. We were college sweethearts and were so happy in the early years. We had all the same interests, loved all the same things, and had the same goals. We fit like a glove. As our careers flourished, so did we. The house got bigger, the cars more expensive, and our family grew. I was happy to take some time off to have the babies, play at-home mom for a while, while each grew to be school-age. Once all three of the kids were in school full-time, I decided to go back to work. I took a position in a firm that allowed me flexible hours so that I could work around the school schedule. All the while, Mark was building his career and climbing the ladder. I supported him all the way, as he did me. Together, we were a force to be reckoned with. As the children grew, I was able to maneuver my schedule around them while maintaining my career and climbing the ladder myself, and I eventually became a partner in my firm.

As I was driving to my new life, I could not help but to relive all those years—the family outings, the family vacations, and the events for the kids and our companies. When did things change?

Neither one of us could pinpoint the exact time. Honestly, neither one of us even noticed. We were happy with our life together that we had worked so hard to build. Mark would stay that way forever if he had his choice. I just could not continue to live a mediocre life, going through the motions day by day by day. I wanted more!

As I drove on, I could feel myself getting stronger and more focused. All my doubt was starting to wash away. I was starting to believe that I had done the right thing for me although I could not help but to wonder about the long last effects of my actions. My children had not spoken to me since I announced that I was leaving a week earlier. Mark walked out of the room, and I found him crying later. He did not want to discuss it with me, saying that he never saw it coming and did not understand how I could do something like this to him or our family.

I tried to convince myself that once the initial shock had worn off, they would come around. Or maybe that was wishful thinking. All I knew is that after nearly thirty years of marriage, I was on my own. I had no one to answer to, no one to take care of, but also no one to talk to about how I was feeling about my newfound freedom. This was the first time in my life that I truly felt alone.

I drove the two hours to my new home, a small studio apartment in the booming metropolis of Portsmouth, New Hampshire. The entire ride was full of mixed emotions running from excitement about my new journey, to sadness about how I left things, and then panic about being on my own with no one to lean on. Mark had been my rock for all these years, and although our relationship was not the way it once was, he had always been my go-to for everything, good, bad, and indifferent. It was going to be a huge adjustment to learn to be able to handle everything on my own.

As I pulled up to my new building, I could not help but think of how in just a couple of hours my life had made a drastic change; was I ready for this? But it was too late now to go back as the bomb was released.

I parked my Mercedes SUV next to the Subaru wagons and Hondas in the parking lot of my new building. The building was an old factory that had been renovated to house modern studio apartments for up-and-coming artists and professionals. Not at all what I was used to. Our house is a four-bedroom, five-bathroom modern colonial in a well-established suburban neighborhood where everyone knows everyone but keeps their respective distances. This was definitely going to be a different way of life for me. I guess if you are going to do something, do it all the way.

As I walked through the modern front foyer of the building, with its coffee nook areas of oversized leather chairs and café tables and slate floors, I could not help but think that I was not sure that I fit in here. Maybe once long ago as an aspiring grad student, working to get my Juris Doctorate and to be the next upcoming judge, but not at this stage of my life. I again could not help but to wonder if this was just craziness on my part or a midlife crisis or something.

I took the elevator to the fourth floor, and as the doors opened, I froze. I was not able to move my legs or even my hands to stop the doors from closing. I don't know what came over me, but it felt like taking that first step through the elevator doors onto the floor of my new home was just too much. Instead, I rode the elevator back down to the lobby. As it stopped on each floor, someone else got onto the elevator. I smiled an awkward smile, knowing that all those twenty-somethings were thinking that I was someone's mother visiting from out of town.

I waited for everyone to exit the elevator, took a deep breath, and hit the button for the fourth floor again. I promised myself that I would actually get off the elevator this time.

As the doors opened, I stepped off. I walked slowly to the door to my new apartment, 4E, and I opened the door. The apartment was beautiful in its rustic-modern-meets-industrial look. High ceilings that house the ductwork for the floor were all painted black to hide in plain sight. The exterior walls were brick with spots of plaster over them as if someone tried to clean them up and make them brighter but just gave up. The interior walls were a muted shade of lavender that was not something that I would have chosen, but that caught my eye as appealing.

There were no furnishings yet. I did not want to take anything from the house as Mark and the kids were still there. I also did not want any of the memories that came with any of those furnishings. Or the guilt. No, I will go shopping and make an entirely fresh start.

While I was the one that decorated our home and bought all the interior furnishings, with our money, of course, they were not mine. This time, I could decorate, and it will all be just mine. I could even buy flowered bedding or pink if I wanted that. Not that I would actually want anything pink, but it was entirely my decision.

That first night, I ordered sushi from the little place down the street and walked down to pick it up. The city streets were warm; the glow of the streetlights on the paver stone streets make me wonder if one day there had been carriages and horses where I was walking.

I walked home and ate my sushi alone. I then set up the few items that I had brought with me and slept on the floor in my new room on an air mattress. I would have to try to get out and order furniture as soon as I could in the morning to make sure that I did not have to spend too many nights on the floor. I pretended that it was a campout like we once did on Friday and Saturday nights with the kids when they were little. The only thing missing was Mark, the kids, the explosion of blankets and pillows, and s'mores. I could not help but feel a pang of disappointment. I quickly brushed it away and started to plan the next day. I wanted to do some exploring and some shopping.

As I tried to fall asleep, my mind wandered back to earlier when I was leaving and no one came out of the house. Were they going about the rest of the day as if it were any other day? Were they all crying and sitting around eating ice cream trying to make sense of this? Part of me wanted to call and check on everyone, but the other part felt like I needed to maintain my position. I had made a decision, and I needed to stick to it. That nagging question continued to come into my mind. Was it the right decision?

Whether it was the right one or wrong one, the decision was made, the damage was done, and I needed to move on from here. I just was not sure how to do that or where here was.

There was nothing like waking up in your new place after the first night. Getting out of bed and wandering around your new house or apartment was an amazing feeling. It had been so many years since I had felt this feeling; I was like a kid at Christmas. I took in the view from my floor-to-ceiling industrial-sized windows that looked out onto the city and the river just a few blocks beyond. The streets were already active with people out shopping and grabbing their morning coffee. It was a Thursday morning, so there were also those morning commuters trying to get to their jobs. I had decided to move up in the middle of the week so that I could have a few days to get myself and my new apartment together before I had to start my new job on Monday morning.

Leaving my partnership and the firm with which I had worked for the past fifteen-plus years was almost as hard as leaving my family. Thankfully, everyone was very understanding and had nothing but wonderful things to say when I left. I had also left with a provision to my partnership contract that I could return within the next five years if my new venture did not work out as long as I had not been employed in any competition with my former firm. That was not going to be a problem as I was leaving the legal field. The licensing to move from Connecticut to New Hampshire would have been quite a headache, and I felt like I needed a break from the law for a while.

I took a position in the law department at the local college. I would be working with students to prepare them for law school in their pursuit of a graduate degree. The university needed someone with legal experience that could help to prepare students for not only law school but the expectations after law school, such as taking and passing the bar and becoming a practitioner. It sounded like the perfect blend for my experience and would get me out of the grind of the day-to-day as a lawyer.

That would mean that I have the next four days to furnish my new apartment, learn the area, shop to stock my kitchen, and unpack so that I can be ready to start work on Monday. I had my work cut out for me.

My first order of business was to get dressed and find coffee. I wished that I had brought a coffee maker, cup, and the fixings for the perfect morning coffee, but with the strain of leaving the house, it slipped my mind, and I had not thought that far ahead. I would have loved to have just sipped my coffee watching the city and enjoying the peace and quiet of this moment.

I dragged the last few boxes from my car up to the apartment, got dressed for my day of shopping, and set out to find the coffee shop that I had heard some of my neighbors in the elevator mention. It turned out that it was a lovely little coffee shop around the corner, overlooking a little square. It was the typical fast-paced shop that you see in the movies with the staff yelling people's names and orders that no one could understand. It smelled like heaven and intrigued me. It was perfect. I ordered a coffee, or what I hoped was coffee, and a scone and waited for my name to be yelled, signaling me that my order was ready.

I grabbed my goods and went out to sit on a bench in front of the coffee shop to people watch. I was not disappointed. There was an eclectic mix of people, young and old. There appeared to be very artsy people with clothes that flowed with color and comfort who seemingly glided down the street and people in suits and business attire walking with purpose. I was rather enjoying the show and my breakfast when my phone rang. I had almost forgotten that I had it with me. When I looked down and saw Mark's name on the screen I froze. For a moment, I forgot where I was and hesitated to answer.

I picked up and answered, "Hello?"

There was a moment of silence before I heard Mark say, "I was not sure if you would even answer."

"Neither was I" was all that I could say.

After a few awkward moments, Mark went on to ask questions about where things were in the house and how to do things like start the laundry and how much soap to use. I provided him with instructions on these things.

Then he asked "So how are you? Are you okay? I assume you made it up there alright."

All I could muster for a response was "I'm good." I did not even know what else to say to him. This man and I had spent the last thirty-plus years of my life with, and I did not know how to talk to him or what to say.

With the awkward silence, he said "Well, thank you for your help. Have a good rest of your day" and ended the call.

I sat staring at my phone, hoping that every conversation with him was not going to be that hard. How could we be here when we have three children and an extensive past together? But then again, what did I expect? I just shattered his life to start my own new life. Did I really think we were going to still be friends?

I sat eating the rest of my breakfast with that sinking feeling in the pit of my stomach, just wanting it to go away so I could enjoy my new surroundings and my new life.

Through the rest of the day shopping and picking out things for my new place, I could not help but think about that conversation and how uneasy I was feeling. I should be excited that I was starting a new chapter in my life and I was on my own, making my own decisions, with no one dictating anything. I was the master of my own universe. But are we ever really our own bosses? There is always something that dictates what we can and cannot do in our lives.

As kids, we pushed to be grown-up so we can stay up late and eat whatever we want and, the big one…not go to school. Then we became adults, and we wished we were kids again, going back to a time of no responsibility or work. We realized that our lives were still dictated by laws and rules, jobs and bosses, and our finances. We were not actually able to do anything we wanted at all. Add to that the pull of those around us. I had never felt that I could do whatever I wanted as I had someone questioning me. Are you really going to wear that out? Do we really want that car? Are you sure we can afford to take the time off for that vacation? With all that gone, I can make my own choices.

I was able to order my new furniture, bought new bedding and drapery, and grocery shopped for myself for the week. It would be the first time that I could experiment with foods and tastes and not have to worry about what the other members of my family would or would not eat. I could also choose to order takeout if I wanted to do that.

By day two, things were still going well. The apartment was coming along, having had most of the furniture delivered and in place. I was finally going to be able to sleep on something other than the floor. The walls had decoration, my kitchen was set up, and I was feeling much more at home. I decided to take a break from moving and took a walk farther into the city. I was taking in the people, the shops, and the cafés of downtown. I found lovely little specialty shops where I was able to get things like imported olive oils and freshly baked bread, both of which I would use later to make myself a snack.

I walked a little farther and found the waterfront. I stopped to watch the boats going by and the people at the restaurants overlooking the water. I could not help but to think of Mark and our mutual love for this type of atmosphere. When we were young and in love, we would walk along the piers back in Connecticut, talking about how some day we would own a boat of our own and cruise to destinations that we read about in books. Sadly, our suburban life took over, and that dream never became a reality. When I mentioned that to him years ago, he laughed and told me how impractical that idea was and that we had just been young and crazy.

It still tugged at my heart that I was not able to share this experience with him. I walked back home thinking about how different I had thought our life would be when we first started out. Somehow, while life was happening, we lost sight of all the things that we had once discussed and how we expected things to go. As our children came along and we purchased our home, moved along in our careers, and became swept away with business meetings and parties, school events, and sports, that all seemed like something we had just read somewhere in a book. Why did we let those dreams go?

As I prepared my dinner and planned to sit down to watch an old love story, I received a text. It was the first one that I had received from any of my children since leaving. It was my oldest son, Daniel, asking how things were with the new place.

Our oldest son was the type of person that just wanted everyone to be happy. He was very laid-back, did not get upset about much, and just always went with the punches. He was away at school and about to graduate. I had hated to call to give him the news, but I did not want to wait until I saw him again as I was afraid that he would hear it from another source before I was able to tell him myself.

I told him that things were coming along and that everything was still pretty new. I asked how school was going and if he was getting ready for graduation. Graduation...that was something I had not thought about. In the rush to get out, move, and start my new position, I had not thought about it. Of course, I knew he was graduating and would be there. But I had not thought about the fact that we would all be there as a family. This included our parents and extended family. We would need to have a graduation party after, which would traditionally be held at our house. How would I make preparations, prepare the house, and host a party in a home that I no longer shared with the family? I was sure that by now, Mark had spoken with his family to tell them what had transpired, and the kids had probably told their friends and grandparents.

I honestly had not thought about telling my parents yet or even my friends, which were really our friends. It may have been because I was afraid that they would tell me I was crazy or try to talk me out of it. Or maybe it was because I did not want the judgment. We were considered a power couple. Our family was the *it* family that everyone loved and admired. I felt that by telling people that I was leaving, I was saying that I had failed somehow or that the appearance was a fake. But it was not. We truly were happy, and so close, and a loving family. It was just not enough. I needed more.

I knew that sounded ridiculous. I wanted and needed more, so I left to be alone. That was not really what I wanted. I just didn't want to be in a relationship, living a life that was not giving me what I needed. I needed fun, some excitement, affection, attention, and someone who wanted to pursue the dreams that we discussed rather than saying that those dreams were ridiculous.

Daniel and I chatted for a bit longer about how school was going, the plan for graduation and the date, and what he was going to do after graduation. Then came the big question.

"Mom, have you talked to Dad?"

I told him that I had talked to him briefly yesterday.

"No, I mean really talked to him? He does not understand why you left, and honestly, neither do I! The girls are angry, but I'm just confused."

Our daughters were very headstrong and did not like change. Jordyn, our middle daughter, was brilliant and currently in her second year of college. Michele had graduated early in December but was to walk with the rest of her class next month for the final graduation ceremony. Again, not great timing on my part as that would be another graduation and party that we would be attending together but separate.

"I know, honey. I am so sorry that this is all so confusing, but it is complicated. Once you are all set with graduation, maybe you can come up to spend a few days with me and we can talk more. Just please don't worry about your father and I right now. We are good. Just get ready to graduate! I am so proud of you! I love you, talk soon!" It sounded convincing, but were we really good?

"I love you too, Mom! Call if you need anything."

I distractedly watched my movie, nibbling on dinner, but I couldn't help but have a terribly sick stomach. I thought about my conversation with Daniel. I was so anxious and excited to just get out of the situation that I really did not think about the entire picture… and yet worrying about all the other factors was exactly what had kept me in my situation for as long as I had been.

By Sunday morning, I was starting to feel like the apartment was home. I had been through my morning routine a couple of times and was working on tweaking the details, like where the coffee was, getting my cup and spoon, and sitting at my little table looking out over the city enjoying my coffee while watching the hustle and bustle of the street. With getting comfortable though came the loneliness that started creeping in. It was just like when the kids were little and we were able to get away for a few days without them. The novelty wore off, and I started to miss them.

While I sipped my coffee, watching the couples and a few families with their little ones, I could not help but wonder what my children were doing. It was Sunday, so Mark would have gone downstairs, grabbed a cup of coffee, and stood at the kitchen island, drinking it while he scrolled the news on his phone. One of the girls would have come in, asked what he was doing and what the plan was for the day, then joined him in a cup of coffee while scrolling through one of their social media sites from the other side of the island. It was all very Hallmark-like and predictable. This was part of what I had left to escape from, and yet I found myself missing the routine of it if not the players.

It's not that I did not love Mark; of course, I still do! We had a long life that we built together; we built a family, and we were partners in all of it for so long. He had become one of, if not my best friend. I shared almost everything with him. That was what made it more difficult that I did not have him to share this experience with. I would normally be calling him to tell him what I had found shopping or describe what I saw on the street or how good the coffee was at the little shop down the street. At one time, we had loved to explore and experience things like this together.

What if he still wanted to experience these things but had felt trapped just like I had. Except he did not leave and I did. What if I had just asked him to make these changes with me? Would he have done it? I mean, realistically, that would not have worked as we both needed to deal with the house and the kids and our bills as well as our respective careers. But what if we had made the steps to change our stagnant life? Would he have done it with me? I may never know because I made that decision for him. Although if I think about it now, I did try. I begged him to do things and go to places, but he was always too busy and wrapped up in projects or the kids or helping other people. I had joked about running away from all the craziness that had become our life and hiding, and he had every reason why that would never work. So to be fair, I did ask in an offhanded way. Plus, there was the issue of him not trying to stop me when I said I was going. Even if I had caught him off guard and he was a bit stunned by my announcement, my first reaction would have been to tell him to stay. Why didn't he tell me to stay or try to stop me?

As I thought about all this, sipping my coffee, watching the city go by, my phone ringing startled me. I was a little surprised to see that Mark was calling. I hesitated to answer.

"Hello?"

After nearly thirty seconds of silence, Mark said, "Hey…I was not sure you would answer."

"Well, of course, I would answer! Why wouldn't I?"

"I'm not sure. I thought maybe you hated me and that was why you ran."

"I didn't run. I walked slowly…so how are things there? Are the girls okay? Are you okay?"

"Everything is fine. Weird but fine. The girls miss you, but they are confused and angry right now."

"I was expecting that, but I don't think I was fully prepared for it. Are you angry too?"

"I don't know what I am right now. I'm not feeling much of anything. Confused maybe. Out of sorts that things are just not normal."

"I understand that."

We both sat silent for several minutes, not really knowing what else to say to each other. There was so much that I wanted to say, but I really did not know how to say it. I finally broke the ice and said that I had to go to get things finished up as I was to be starting my new job in the morning and wanted to be fully prepared. Mark wished me well. I thanked him, and then we awkwardly said good-bye. It was the first time that we did not say "I love you" as we hung up. That stung more than I expected.

I busied myself for the rest of the day trying to prepare for my week and the new job and trying to push thoughts of Mark and the kids out of my head. Not in a way like I want to forget them as that could never and would never happen. But more in a way of if I don't get out of my own head about this, I am going to jump in the car and go home and abort the entire mission. I had to keep reminding myself that if I went home, I would just be going back to what I had left, and there was a reason that I had left in the first place. So keeping busy, making this my new home and routine was what I needed to keep doing. I will just hope that as time goes on, things will get easier. Something told me that it was going to get worse before it would get better. I needed to deal with the situation with my girls and try to repair those relationships and deal with Mark about how the future was going to look for both of us. I just needed to get through today then one day at a time.

Monday and the new job were alright. It was very strange going to a new place as I had been with my prior firm for so long. It was even stranger being the lower man on the so-called totem pole and having a supervisor that was half my age. Actually, almost everyone was younger than me. My day consisted of learning my way around campus, finding the best place for coffee and lunch, and getting to understand the computer system. I did not even have the opportunity to dive into exactly what my duties would entail.

By the time that I drove home from work, I was exhausted. It had been a long emotional few days, and this was pretty much the icing on the cake. I stopped for some takeout down the road, along with a bottle of wine. When I got home, I took a hot shower then sat down at the table with a glass of wine and my takeout. As I stared out the window, a sinking feeling came over me. I had no one to share my day with. I could not complain to anyone about dumping a cup of coffee as I was trying to open a door and juggle my manuals. I had no one to talk about how tired I was or how distracted I had become midday when I could not stop thinking about my children and how I had not spoken to them in nearly a week. I don't think I had gone five hours without talking to them, never mind five days. I had no one, and I had no one to blame but myself.

I finished my glass of wine, or liquid courage as I liked to call it, and I picked up my phone. First, I tried calling my middle daughter but got no answer. I knew that she had to be screening my calls because that girl always had her phone in her hand. I left a message, telling her how much I missed her and just wanted to hear her voice. I hung up and thought how fake my voice had sounded being so upbeat and cheerful when I was feeling anything but those things.

I next tried calling my youngest daughter. She picked up on the first ring but did not speak. "Hello? Hello? Are you there? Can you hear me? It's Mom!"

I heard her moving around, but she was not talking.

"Baby, I just called to tell you that I love and miss you. I would understand if you are not ready to talk to me, but I am thinking about you."

Then she hung up. I guess it was progress that she picked up at all.

I wanted to call Mark, but every time that I tried to dial the phone, I just could not hit send. I had to keep remembering that I had chosen this. I left, not him. I could not keep pulling him back in any time that I questioned my actions. I also could not admit defeat. Even if that was what I was feeling, defeated!

I was too tired or sad, I'm not sure which, to do anything more, so I decided to go to bed. I took a book with me in the hopes that I could read enough to maybe fall asleep. Shortly into my second page, my phone vibrated. It was Jordyn texting. My heart skipped a beat, and I was unsure what to expect as I opened my phone. It said simply, "I got your message." Nothing more! There was no "I love you" or "I miss you" or anything more. I waited to see if she would send anything more but wanted to keep the lines of communication open, so I texted back, "I'm glad. I miss you!" I waited another ten minutes, but there was no response. I had to believe that her not telling me to go away or never talk to her again was good. I decided to just simply text "Good night."

As I lay there, staring at the ceiling in my new apartment, I could think of nothing more than my children and how much I had broken them. I did not know how to fix them without breaking myself. Was that selfish as a parent? Are we not supposed to protect our children at all costs? But did that cost have to be ourselves? I would jump in front of a speeding car or a bullet for my children. I just don't know if I could live my life for them. Was that wrong?

In the days and weeks that followed, I continued to struggle to become familiar with my new duties at work and my now lonely life at home. I continued to reach out to the girls to tell them how much I loved them and missed them and that I hoped that they would forgive me.

Talking to Mark was still strained, but we spoke nearly daily, if not by phone then by text. We were awkwardly trying to navigate through planning for Daniel's graduation and party, and I was dreading the thought of returning to that house with the way things were at the moment with everyone. Mark was putting on a brave face and being very gracious about including me and allowing me to help with all the preparations. I mean he was my son, too, but under the circumstances, this could have gone much differently. Mark even asked if I would prefer to have a small gathering in a restaurant with just immediate family to celebrate. But I did not want to punish my son or diminish his accomplishment because I felt the need to make a life change.

Ultimately, we agreed to family, immediate friends, and friends of Daniel's that would hopefully distract everyone else from the fact that I was there but not living at home. I had not yet told anyone, and I did not know who Mark or the kids had told yet. I was still trying to grasp the reality of all of it, so I was not sure how to explain it to anyone else. I think part of me was still afraid of anyone else's opinions as well.

I asked Mark how the girls were doing whenever we spoke, and he was always very vague with his response. They were good was all he could say. We would need to make arrangements for Michele's graduation party as well, but when I brought it up, Mark brushed it aside saying "Let's get through one party at a time." The first few times he did it, I had to agree. One party was more than enough for me at the moment. Still, I could not help but wonder what that meant and whether we were ever going to talk about it.

The following week, we watched our son graduate. I made my entrance to the facility a little late to avoid any scene with the girls if I were to try to sit with everyone. I snuck into the back and found a seat near the group. When I was asked, I would just explain that I had been stuck in traffic. The ceremony was like any other, and I cried watching my son walk across that stage for the last time. He was now a full-grown man and would be making his own life decisions from now on. I just hoped that he would be happy.

After the ceremony, everyone got up and left the auditorium. I slowly made my way out to where all the graduates were congregating. I spotted Daniel, and as I walked toward him, I saw my daughters and Mark running to him to congratulate him. I hesitated, and Mark saw me stop. It was the first time that we had seen each other since before I left. I gave him a half smile. We could not look away from each other. I eventually broke our gaze after what seemed like an eternity but in reality was probably only about thirty seconds. I heard "What is she doing here?" and I looked up to see Jordyn looking at me with disgust.

Daniel looked at her and said "She is here to celebrate *me*!" and walked toward me with arms out. "Hi, Mom!"

I immediately started crying and walked to hug him. That hug was more than I realized that I needed. The love and compassion and comfort of someone I loved. I had been trying so hard to be tough and strong to make my own decision and stick with it that I had not realized what I was lacking.

I could hear the underhanded comments coming from my daughters as we hugged. Then I heard Mark's stern but soft voice say, "She is still your mother. Show her respect. This is your brother's day and not the place or time!"

As much as I appreciated the sentiment, part of me wanted to turn around and tell him that I didn't need his saving…even though I did, and at that moment, I was grateful. My in-laws greeted me with cold "How are you doing?" greetings to which I responded just as briefly.

With all that out of the way, we made our way back to the house. I took the long way, trying to delay the inevitable as long as possible. I had not been to the house since I left, and I was extremely apprehensive to be back. I did not know how I was going to feel pulling in the driveway again or seeing everyone there. Even worse, I was going back for a party that I was not throwing in a home that was no longer mine for one of my children. We raised the kids in that house. We lived as a family in that house for nearly thirty years. Yet I was no longer a part of that household.

As I pulled in the driveway, it was as if nothing changed. Everything looked exactly as I had left it. The lawn and hedges were manicured. The garbage cans were where they always were, and the welcome flag still flew out front. I am not sure what I was expecting. It was just me that left. Did I think that the house was going to crumble and fall down? Life still goes on after you are gone! I walked up the stairs thinking of the irony in the flag waving "welcome." Was I though?

I was not sure whether I should knock or just walk in. After all, it was not my house anymore. I was saved from the dilemma by Daniel walking out to get something from his car and holding the door open for me.

"Oh, hi, Mom," he said as he brushed past me, just as he had done a thousand times before, like nothing had changed. Thank God for that kid or I probably would have driven home to New Hampshire by now.

I hesitantly walked in and up the stairs to the kitchen from the breezeway. The kitchen was bustling with activity. Mark and the girls were putting together the food and laying out the paper plates and cups. I heard Jordyn say, "I don't know where to put any of this. Mom usually takes care of it all."

As I stepped in, I took my cue and said, "Well, I can show you if you want."

Everyone instantly froze at the sound of my voice. Mark turned slowly to look at me.

"I'm sorry, Daniel let me in. I hope that was okay" was all I could think to say.

"Of course, it is okay. It is your house too" was his reply.

Ouch, that smarted a little, but not nearly as much as the look on the girls' faces. I could have sworn that for a moment, I saw relief or excitement or something similar to that. Oh, how I missed the look when I would come home from work and they saw me. It was always "Mom…I have something to tell you" or "Mom, I need help" or "Mom, where is my…" Now, it was a look of confusion and hurt and betrayal when they looked at me.

I stepped forward toward them. "Here, let me show you."

I took the plates from Jordyn's hand and picked up the utensils and headed out onto the back deck to help set up. The girls grabbed items and followed. Maybe this was the icebreaker we needed.

The evening went as well as could be expected considering I was in a situation of my own creation and no one knew how to feel or react to it. I said my goodbyes fairly early as I had a two-plus hour drive to make. Mark walked me out to my car in spite of my reluctance.

"Thank you for coming. It meant a lot to Daniel...and me."

"Well, of course, I would come! I did not stop being a mother just because...well, you know what I mean."

"What do you mean? Is this really over, Laura? Are we really over?"

As he took a step closer, I could feel my body grow rigid. I did not want to be having this conversation here, with all these people in our house...his house, with our children here. I did not want to be having this conversation at all, honestly.

"I'm sorry, I am tired, and I have a long drive. And you have a party to go back to. Good night, Mark." I had to turn away so that he could not see the tears streaming down my face.

"Good night, Laura...I...drive safe." He turned and walked back to the house as I got into my car and started to back down the driveway. As I glanced back, I saw him standing with his hand on the doorknob, watching me drive away...again.

Driving home, I could not get out of my own head. I replayed my leaving (both times) over and over, wondering if I were doing the right thing. Had I tried hard enough to make my needs and wants known? What if I had been more vocal or thrown a fit to make myself heard? But would it have mattered? The flip side of that was why didn't I? If something is wrong in the house, you mention it and try to figure out a solution. This should have been the same. I should have been more urgent in my mentioning that we needed to have more us time, that I wanted to go on vacation and get away, and that it was necessary. I made excuses like our lives were too busy or we just cannot get away because we have this event or who can we get to come and stay with the kids that can handle all their activities.

My focus should have been in making it happen. I made everything else happen. This was the most important thing, and I should have made it happen. Instead, I ran. I didn't solve anything. In fact, I just made a mess of things. It was not that I didn't want my family life or Mark or our amazing life anymore. It was that I just wanted it to slow down and not be so crazy. The timing was ridiculous on my part. Our children were almost all grown and out of the house, so inevitably, our life would have been slowing down. So what made me go now?

I continued to beat myself up during the remainder of my drive home, listening to '80s music that brought me back to our early years, singing at the top of my lungs and crying my eyes out. It was sad, therapeutic, and pathetic all at once. By the time I reached my apartment, I looked like I had been in a fight, and I was completely spent from the entire experience.

I continued to reach out to the girls daily for the next couple of weeks. I also continued to speak with Mark on a daily basis. I used the excuse that we needed to plan Michele's graduation party and that I wanted to be a part of it this time. It was, of course, my last child's high school graduation party. It was a huge milestone for her and for us.

We planned everything the way that I had done every prior party, right down to every last detail. As the day approached, I realized that I had always done things over the course of a couple of days. Logistically, with my living two-plus hours away, that was going to be very difficult. Mark offered to have me stay at the house for the period that I needed to be in town to prepare for the party, attend the ceremony itself, and then the day of the party. I was really uncertain about taking him up on the offer. I was not sure what I was so afraid of. Was I afraid that it would be awkward or that I would not want to leave?

I was still incredibly attracted and drawn to Mark. We had always had such an amazing attraction to each other. Since I left, I have tried hard not to think about that or allow it to sway me in any way. It was really difficult being near him at Daniel's graduation party, just seeing him with the kids and taking care of everything. He was so handsome, and had a sense of humor that drew everyone to him. The attraction was not the issue. It was what I felt that I was lacking…attention.

I know that all relationships evolve from passion and not being able to be away from your partner to the day-to-day responsibilities and exhaustion at the end of the day. I have tried to remind myself of that for years. However, fighting for attention daily and going to bed wondering if the person that you are lying next to loves and wants you because they cannot live without you emotionally or if they just need you to wash their socks, now that is not fair. I cried myself to sleep so many nights wondering what was wrong with me that he could not take twenty minutes out of his day to sit on the back deck to watch the sunset over a glass of wine and just talk.

Now, I have broken free from that feeling, and I cannot remember exactly why. More importantly, if I were to go back, even for just a couple of days, would I be able to leave again? I told Mark that I appreciated the offer, but I had to see how I could work out taking time off work since this was a new position. I could not tell him that I was afraid to be in the house with him again and that I might break my resolve. Part of me was excited when he sounded disappointed that I did not say yes right away.

Ultimately, I did take him up on the offer, telling him that it would be so much easier to be able to be there to help put it all together. I also stressed that I needed to be able to sleep in the spare room. He, of course, graciously agreed that he would set up the spare room for me. He also would take care of breaking the news to the girls who were still not returning my messages or calls.

I was torn between feeling like a schoolgirl with a crush and dreading the weekend, not understanding how I could have feelings of excitement when I had made the choice to leave. The heart really is quite confusing and sometimes so in contradiction to your head!

When the day came, I had a hard time deciding what I wanted to bring to wear and fussed over how I looked in everything. I was not normally one that was really worried about how I dressed as I pretty much wore the same thing all the time. I did not know what had come over me. I was going back to the house where we raised our children, to my family to celebrate my daughter's accomplishment. Why was I feeling like I was going on a first date?

I finally just threw some clothes into my overnight bag, locked up my door, and headed to the car. I decided that I could use a little walk before the drive, so I walked to the coffee shop to grab a coffee. As I was standing in line looking around at all the twenty- and thirty-somethings all mingling and talking, I was taken back to when Mark and I were dating in college. We would walk every Saturday and Sunday morning to a coffee shop just off campus to just sit and talk for hours. I smiled at the thought when I heard a voice from next to me say, "Penny for your thoughts."

I was startled and looked around to see a very handsome gentleman who was probably midforties. I said, "Oh, I was just thinking that I remember when I was their age."

We both laughed saying how our twenties were very different from their twenties.

I ordered my coffee as we chatted about time and how it had changed from our youth to now. He introduced himself, "I'm John. I live in the neighborhood. I have seen you around a lot recently, so I'm guessing that you live in the area too?"

"I just moved in down the street," I replied.

"Well, welcome to the neighborhood! I hope to see you around again soon!"

With that, he took his coffee and headed for the door. "I do too," I called after him.

I walked back to the car thinking how odd it was that I had not met anyone since I moved here, and then suddenly, when I was in such turmoil about my feelings for Mark and our current situation, I would suddenly meet someone that piqued my interest. Of course, not that I had any intention of pursuing him or any relationship for that matter. Just odd timing.

When I got to the car, I realized that I had left my phone with my bag. I had three missed calls from Mark. I frantically called him back thinking that something was terribly wrong as I had only been gone about fifteen minutes.

He answered, "Where have you been? I have been trying to call! I'm sorry, that is none of my business. We have a problem."

My heart sank. Please don't tell me that something happened with the kids. "Is everyone alright?"

"Oh, yeah, sorry, everyone is fine! I just got a call from the school, and they had to move the graduation to Saturday instead of Friday, so now the party is going to be the same day at the same time. How can we tell everyone that the party has to be pushed back to later?"

That was his emergency? All I could do was laugh.

"Mark, I had to move so many events at the last minute, that is the easy part! I am on my way home now. We can talk about it when I get there."

As soon as I said it, we both stopped. Home. I said I was coming home. I was hoping that he had not heard it or just didn't make anything of it. I was not so lucky. There was silence on the other end of the phone.

"Hello? Did I lose you?"

"No," he responded. "I was just…ummm…I was just thinking that I am relieved that you can help me to fix this. I mean the party. We can fix the party."

Yep, there it was. He was already analyzing the meaning of my slipup. I was just going to pretend that I had not said it or, at the very least, that it was just part of what I said and we would move on.

"I will see you in a couple of hours. Are the girls home?"

"No, they are out running errands shopping for something to wear to the graduation. I will see you when you get here. Drive safe."

"I will."

As I hung up, I was cursing myself for making an already awkward and difficult situation even worse with my Freudian slip. If that is what that was.

Pulling up to the house this time was less difficult than last time. There were no extra people this time. It did not look like the girls were home yet, and I had already done this once, so that ice was broken. Although I still was not sure whether I should be knocking or just walk in. I decided that I was going to knock out of courtesy. When Mark did not answer right away, I became a bit uncomfortable, feeling like a door-to-door salesman. I called Mark to tell him that I was here. He was in the shower and said to just come in.

I went in and up to the kitchen. It was like nothing had changed since I left. Everything was where it always was. The mail was piling up. He was probably accumulating the bills to pay at the same time of the month. That always drove me nuts. I had to pay them as they came in so they were not so overwhelming. Plus, that way, if something happened, at least they were all up-to-date.

I heard a noise behind me and turned around to find Mark standing there in nothing but a towel. His hair still wet from the shower. "Oh, good, you did get in. I could not remember if I had locked the door. But then you probably still have your key."

It was taking every ounce of willpower for me not to look at his body. That body that I had slept next to for years. The one that I had rarely looked at for the past several years the way that I was looking at him now. Why had I ever stopped looking at that body? When I finally pulled my eyes upward, Mark had a smirk on his face.

"Don't!" I said.

"Don't what?" he said.

"Don't give me that smirk. I was just…surprised, that is all."

"Oh, really? Surprised that I have a body? Because you were staring. By the way, it's not polite to stare!"

"Well, then don't be naked!"

Laughing, he left the room to go get dressed. I went to the kitchen for a cold drink and to try to catch my breath…and some of my dignity back.

Mark returned to the kitchen a few minutes later with more clothes on. We busied ourselves preparing for the coming event and the return of the girls. He helped me take my things to the guest room. Walking past our old room was very strange. It took a lot of concentration for me not to follow my normal routine of walking up the stairs and turning into our room. I could not bring my eyes up from the floor as I walked to the guest room. When I did finally look up, I noticed that he had moved my favorite bedding to the guest room. This was our bedding that I had meticulously picked for us. I looked at him with confusion.

He simply said "I knew it would make you happy" and walked out of the room.

Looking at that bedding, those sheets that we had shared so many nights, I was not sure if it would make me happy. It sounds like such a small ridiculous thing, but it was a memory down a road I was trying so hard to avoid.

As I headed back downstairs, I peeked into our old room. Not much had changed except that he had put our old bedding on the bed. The memories started flooding back, and I had not realized that I had stopped to stare into the room. I heard Mark yell from downstairs, "Are you coming down to help or what?"

Downstairs was a flurry of activity. The girls had come home and were talking up a storm about the dresses they found for graduation and running into friends and who was not talking to who. All the activity stopped when I entered the room. I pretended that it did not hurt and that I had not noticed the glances that they gave Mark.

I piped in with "Let me see what you found for dresses."

They exchanged glances but were excited about their purchases, so they shared them with me and were back to talking up a storm in no time. I glanced up from their conversation to find Mark standing in the corner of the kitchen smiling at us. He and I locked eyes and both smiled. Just as we had done so many times before when the room was full of activity from the kids.

The rest of evening was spent catching up and working on the preparations for the party and graduation. I was filled in on all the gossip that I had missed and heard about every classmate and what to expect with the parents at graduation. Toward the end of the evening, Michele hesitantly asked me how I was doing and what my new place was like. Jordyn shot her a look to which she shrugged and insisted that I tell her. I told her that it was chic, overlooking the city, but it was missing the activity of home.

"Then why did you leave?" asked Michele.

Ouch! I was expecting that question at some point, and honestly, it was not said maliciously as I had expected but more from a place of curiosity and hurt.

"I did not leave you or your sister or brother. I left because I needed to find myself and find what made me happy. I love you all more than I can ever express, but you are all adults and are about to go and find your way in the world too. I felt like it was time for me to find my way."

"But what about dad?"

What about dad? I could not answer that for myself, let alone my child who did not understand why I ripped our family apart. We had the perfect house on the hill, white-picket-fence life, and I destroyed that by leaving. I still was not sure what it was that I was looking for or if I was actually looking for anything. Least of all what I was to do about Mark. I still loved him so much, and after being away from him for the past several weeks, I realized I was also *in* love with him. The two are very different. So what about Mark? I may have destroyed that forever.

"Honey, your father and I are adults, and we will figure things out, but right now, it is about you and your huge accomplishment! Thank you so much for letting me be a part of this! I have really missed you guys." I could not help but to let a few tears fall, and so did they. And just like that, the ice was broken. Now I could only hope that my family was not as broken as I believed we were.

After the girls headed to bed, I was helping Mark clean up the kitchen. We were both pretty quiet, lost in our own thoughts. Then I realized that I did not hear any movement from behind me where Mark had been working to clean off the table as I was filling the dishwasher at the sink. I turned to see him just watching me.

"What are you looking at?" I asked him.

He smiled and said, "Just you doing your thing. I had not realized how much I missed you being in the kitchen."

I looked at him and swatted him with the dishcloth that I was drying my hands on. "You mean you miss me doing the dishes so that you don't have to," I said and laughed.

Mark got quiet and looked down. "Laura, I really miss you! I miss us. I have not known what to do without you. I don't mean with the house or the kids, that is the easy part. I don't know how to be… without you. You are such a huge part of me. I feel like I lost my best friend, and it has left a huge hole."

I walked toward him, wanting to hug him but afraid to. I don't know what I am afraid of…maybe me, maybe I'm afraid that with that hug, I will be sucked back into this life. But would that be so bad? It was a good life. So what was it that I actually wanted? I honestly could not say. Right now, I wanted this, us, him, but I couldn't bring myself to tell him that.

"I know" was all I could muster up to say to him. What the hell was wrong with me?

I put my hand on his back, trying hard not to hug him, and I told him, "I have missed you too. We have been together so long it was like cutting off my arm. So many times I have wanted to call and share something with you, but it was not fair for me to do that to you. Mark, I never meant to hurt you. I know that sounds cliché and that it probably sounds meaningless, but I honestly did not. I needed to do this for me. I felt like I lost myself in all of this." I motioned my arms around the room. "I was a mom, a wife, an attorney, a taxi to practices, a chef, a housekeeper…but I was not me. I have not felt like me for so long that I don't even know who I am anymore. I just did not know how to get to me. I know it was extreme, but I felt like it was the only way."

Mark sat with his head hung down and wrapped his arm around my leg. "Do you still love me?"

My breath was caught in my throat. I wanted to blurt out "Of course, I do!" but I was not sure how that would go. I still did not live here. I had started another life two hours away. I could not just profess my undying love for him and be back just like that.

I looked at him, lifting his face with my hand so he would look at me. "Mark, I have loved you since the day I met you. Nothing will ever change that. We have three beautiful, amazing children together, and we built a lifetime of memories. Nothing can take that away from us. It was never about love. It was about what I needed and did not feel that I was getting."

Mark stared at me for a while until I pulled my hand away. I wanted to step away, but I wanted to wrap my arms around him and have him tell me everything was fine. I was such a mix of emotions. I could tell he wanted to say something more or move toward me as well. As we stood awkward in the moment, we were saved by the bell. The phone ringing to be specific. It was our son, Daniel.

I picked up the phone.

"Hey, Mom, it's me."

"Hi, Daniel, what's up."

"So I just drove by the house, and I had to ask, are you there?"

I told him that I was and that we were preparing for his sister's graduation and the party.

"Oh, cool. Are you okay? Does it feel weird being back there? My sisters are not giving you trouble, are they? I remember how things went at my graduation."

I assured him that I was fine, that the girls were good, and that we had made some headway tonight. I thanked him for being concerned, told him I would see him tomorrow, and that I loved him.

"I love you too, Mom. And tell Dad I said hi!"

As I hung up, I turned to look at Mark. "Just Daniel checking up on me. He saw the car and wondered why I was down."

"Yeah, I figured as much. Well, I'm going to hit the sack. Are you all set for the night?"

"Yeah, I think I'm good. I'm pretty tired myself. It was a long day. See you in the morning."

As Mark turned to walk away, he turned back and said "I love you, Laura. I always will" and walked up the stairs.

I grabbed a glass of water and headed up to my room. I pushed myself past the door to our room that Mark had left ajar. We always closed our door at night, so I had to wonder why he left it open, but I did not want to ask. It could be dangerous for both of us. Once settled into my room, I heard Mark's footsteps quietly coming down the hall. I heard a soft knock on my door. I steadied my breathing to sound like I was sleeping. After a couple of minutes, I heard him head back to his room. As much as I wanted to let him in, I just could not. I did not want to go down that road. I had just escaped from here. Our girls were just next door. Would he expect me to stay? This could not be healthy for either of us. It was better that we just continued to get along and work through this…whatever this was.

The next morning, I came downstairs to Mark sitting at the table in his usual spot drinking his coffee and scrolling through his phone.

"Good morning, sleepyhead. How did you sleep?"

"Okay, I guess. I was up and down." I grabbed my coffee and went to my usual spot. It was like I had never left.

We decided to go try to finish preparations for the party together. We could run all our errands and get things done quicker if one was grabbing what we needed while the other was listing off the items.

It felt odd being back in town and being with Mark doing the things we had once done together. Apparently, I was not the only one who thought it was odd. We ran into several people who looked quite surprised to see us together. I was getting really tired of saying, "Well, our baby girl is graduating, so it's a big milestone for us both!"

After our third stop and the third time I felt the need to defend my presence, we got back into the car with our loot. Mark turned to me and said, "You do not need to defend why you are here to anyone. You belong here, so stop feeding them!"

He turned to start the car, and I could not stop looking at this beautiful man sitting next to me. This man that I quite obviously took for granted. At that particular moment, I could not remember why I had left.

Mark just continued to look ahead and started chuckling, saying, "Stop staring at me, you're creeping me out." He had a knack for making me laugh. Another reason I loved him so much.

The rest of the afternoon was filled with Dunkin'-fueled shopping and laughing and just enjoying the occasion and each other's company.

Saturday, graduation day, was a beautiful early summer day. I was getting myself dressed and ready in a cute little summer dress that I had picked up at a boutique in Portsmouth. I was doing my hair when Michele knocked and came into my room to borrow something.

"*Wow*, Mom, what happened?"

I looked down. "What? What's wrong? Is it ripped?" I spun trying to see myself.

"No, you look amazing! You've never dressed like that before!"

"Oh, stop, of course, I did!"

"No, Mom, you did not! You have always dressed kind of conservatively. Not at all like this. You look *hot*!"

"I do not! What do you want anyway?"

"Now I don't remember." She laughed and bounced out of the room.

I finished my hair, and as I looked in the mirror I thought, *I do look different!*

I headed downstairs, and as I got to the bottom of the stairs, Mark heard me coming and turned around. "*Wow,*" he exhaled slowly. "Look at you, hot momma!"

I laughed and said, "What is with you and your daughter? I'm just wearing a sundress!"

Mark stared saying, "Yeah, but not like anything you have ever worn before. You look amazing!"

"Why, thank you kind sir," I said as I curtsied to him. We both laughed.

Jordyn came running down the stairs, yelling, "Let's go, we are going to be late!" She stopped when she saw me and said "Wow, Mom, you look great. Nice dress!" and then headed toward the door with Michele on her heels. I looked at Mark and said "Someone should have told me how badly I dressed!"

Once at the field where they were holding graduation, there was a sea of people that I was not anxious to see. I knew there would be a lot of questions and snide comments behind my back. Mark must have sensed my anxiety because he walked over and put his hand on my shoulder.

"Laura, it will be fine. Just remember what I said yesterday. You don't have to justify yourself to anyone! Now, let's go watch our little girl graduate!" With that he put his arm out for me to loop mine into, and off we went.

The ceremony was like any other, long and boring, but our girl received several awards for which we could be heard throughout the event. As I sat and watched Mark looking so proud and thinking about what *we*, as a team, accomplished, I was so proud of us. He was beaming from ear to ear when he saw Michele down on the floor. I could not help but to tear up. I was so proud of her, too, but honestly could not keep my eyes off Mark.

The party went well even if it were a bit awkward. I tried to ignore the odd stares and small conversations that stopped as I walked by. I went about my hostess duties as if it were any other event held at our home. Even if it was not "our" home anymore. Mark was amazing as usual. He kept asking how I was doing and if I needed anything throughout the night. I told him I was good and things were going as planned.

As we were cleaning up after all the guests had left, I noticed Mark quietly pretending to do something, but he looked lost in thought.

"Hey," I said. "Are you okay?"

He shook his head as if to clear it and chuckled. "I'm fine, sorry, I'm just tired and probably just daydreaming. Or night dreaming as it really is past my bedtime."

I shook my head. "Oh yeah, I remember. You always fall asleep at eight on the couch. I could never hear my show because of your snoring," I said as I continued to wipe down the counter. It was quiet, so I turned around.

Mark was just looking at me with tears in his eyes. "I miss you, Laura."

I just stood there, looking at this beautiful man that I promised to love and cherish until death do us part. This man who had been my best friend for more than half my life, the father of my children, my rock for years, and my heart. I had broken him. This reality hit like a freight train. While I was working to try to figure out how to find me, I had lost a huge piece of me. How would I ever repair that? How do I even try to? But the bigger and harder question…do I want to? Do I want to go back to what I was not having found what I was looking for? Or had I found it in the realization that maybe it was right here all along?

I did not know what to say to him. I was in my own head thinking that if I say what I want to, that I miss him too, that I was sorry, and can he forgive me, maybe we could just go back to what we had. But I was not sure that was exactly what I wanted. At least maybe not yet. On the other hand, not saying anything or saying something other than "I miss you too" could mean the end of us, and I was not sure that I was ready for that or wanted that.

Instead, I simply said, "I know, I'm sorry." The hurt in his eyes showed me that I had made the wrong decision. I quickly followed with "I never meant to hurt you, Mark. You mean so much to me, and everything that we had means the world to me. I just need to figure this out."

He looked at me, and after several minutes, he said, "You said 'had,' everything we had. Is this over? Are we over?"

I could not look at him. I did not want him to see me cry because I did not want pity or for him to try to fix things like he always does. So I simply turned slightly away from him and said, "Well, I don't live here anymore, so I don't know."

Well, that was not at all how I feel. I wanted to run to him and wrap my arms around him and tell him to please forgive me and that I have never stopped loving him. I was just terrified of going back to what we were, and all this would have been for nothing.

Again I heard no movement behind me. When I was able to regain my composure, I turned around to look at him. He was just staring at me, no words, no emotions, like he was numb. All he said was, "No, I guess you don't live here anymore." Then he slowly turned around and started walking toward the stairs and called over his shoulder, "I will finish cleaning up in the morning. You don't need to do anymore. Thank you for the help today." With that, he headed up the stairs and to our room…his room.

What had I done? While I'm figuring myself out, I may have very well destroyed the best thing in my life. I most certainly have hurt the most amazing man that I have ever known. I was not sure it was even possible to come back from this. Honestly, I never expected to be at this point where I was able to come back to the house after I had left the way that I did. This was like a second chance, and I was pretty sure that I just blew that chance.

Mark said to leave the mess, but in my present state of mind, I could not just go to sleep. Instead, I busied myself with cleaning up the kitchen, putting all the food away, vacuuming, and mopping everything so that in the morning, it would be as if the party had never happened. I had destroyed our relationship; this was the least I could do for him.

After I was done, I turned out all the lights, locked the doors, and headed up to bed like I had thousands of times before. Except this time was probably the last time I would ever do it in this house.

I lay in bed trying not to think about things and instead was busying my mind with thoughts of the coming week and what I had going on at work. I decided to check my email to see if there was anything new from mail. After a few minutes, I got a text. It was Mark.

"I'm sorry for whatever I have done to make you want to run away from me. I am sorry for whatever I have done to make you stop loving me. But I want you to know that I love you. I have always loved you, and I *will* always love you. Good night, Laura."

At this point, I was sobbing. I had no idea how to respond to this. It was never Mark that was the problem. It was never that I stopped loving him. How could you explain that to someone when you had left them and turned their entire world upside down? I was trying to decide if I should just pretend to be sleeping and that I had not seen the message or if I should respond. While I was contemplating how to handle the situation, I received another text. "You do not need to respond. I just needed you to know."

I decided that the best way, for now, to handle it was to think about it overnight and make a decision in the morning.

Sleep did not come easily, or really at all. I kept replaying the last six months over and over in my mind, even the period before I left. I had not been happy for some time, and I had convinced myself that Mark had not been happy either. But maybe I was wrong. I had also believed that I was leaving because Mark was suffocating me. Looking back now, it could have been that I just did not see another way to get away from the feeling of being trapped. I just didn't know what I was trapped in. I had everything that I had always wanted: a beautiful home; a loving, devoted husband; beautiful and amazing children; a career; and an incredible social life. So what made me feel trapped? And why do I suddenly not remember that trapped feeling at all?

Now, not only had I destroyed my family, but I had deeply hurt the only man that I have ever loved and still love with all of my heart. I could honestly say that now I feel trapped in a situation of my own choosing and in a life that I have now created for myself while my family continued to live out my dream life.

Lying there for hours, beating myself up over my decisions, which now seemed so rash and not well-thought-out, I cried for myself. My only hope of fixing this was to get myself together and be honest with Mark. In order to do that, I had to be very raw and vulnerable, and I was not sure that I could do that yet.

When I heard movement in the house, I decided that I had wallowed in my own self-pity for long enough. I got up, got dressed, and tried to lessen the swelling in my eyes as much as I could with cold water and makeup.

I eventually made my way downstairs to where I was expecting to see Mark sitting at the table in his usual spot with his coffee and paper. Instead it was Michele just making her way in from her morning run. "Oh, good morning, Mom!"

"Good morning, honey. I was expecting to see your father."

She looked at me and said, "Oh, Dad left early this morning. He said something about needing to get to a jobsite for a quick look at something that he was supposed to look at on Friday but had not had the chance to because of the party prep. He said he should be back by early afternoon but was not sure he would see you before you left. Do you have to head back early or can you stick around for a while?"

I was not going to lie, that news hurt. I knew that Mark did not have any work that he had to do on Friday because we joked about how his phone was so quiet while we were shopping all day, but it had never been when I was home. He was avoiding me, and that did not feel good at all. Maybe he was giving me a taste of what he was feeling, or maybe he was trying to start to forget me. I knew I should have responded last night. I hope that was not the last straw for him.

I looked at Michele who was still standing and looking at me waiting for an answer. "Oh, yes, I do need to get back, but I can stay for a little while and have some coffee with you. It will be nice to catch up."

Michele ran off to take a quick shower after her run, and I set about making coffee and trying not to touch my phone. After coffee was made and I was waiting for Michele, I opened my texts to write to Mark. His message from the night before was still open, and "I love you" was all that I could see. I should have just told him then. It was my chance to say "I still love you too, Mark. I always have and always will." What was I thinking? Now that so much time had passed and clearly he was avoiding me, what could I say, "Hey, sorry, I'm an idiot"? I was!

While I was staring at my phone trying to figure out what to say, Mark walked in the door. I nearly dropped my phone with my jaw.

"Hey, there, sleepyhead." Mark chuckled in my direction. "Sorry I was gone when you got up. I didn't want to wake you, but I had to run to a jobsite quickly."

I must have been staring strangely at him because he shot me a strange look back. "Oh, yeah, sorry. I was not expecting to see you, so you caught me off guard. Michele said you were not expecting to be back until this afternoon."

"Yeah, it ended up being much easier than I had expected, so it didn't take me long. How did you sleep?"

"I DIDN'T!" I wanted to scream. "Oh, you know, the normal for me. You?" A little white lie.

"Fine. I was a little restless but exhausted after the last few days…in a good way."

I had to get up to get some coffee just to get my mind off the conversation. He was talking as if nothing had happened. As if he had not poured his heart out and bore his soul of pain to me and I had just kicked it aside like I didn't care. It had to be a defense mechanism or he was testing me or he was sorry that he had said it.

"Oh, hey, Dad," Michele chimed as she bounced into the kitchen. "Mom and I were going to have some coffee and catch up. Do you want to join us?"

"No," said Mark. "I have been able to catch up with Mom over the last few days. You, two, can catch up now. I have some yard work to finish anyway." With that, he glanced at me, winked, and walked upstairs to get changed.

Michele and I sat for a couple of hours catching up on all the gossip with her friends, and she wanted to know all the cool things about my new place and job. We made plans for her to come and visit for a weekend to get away before the end of summer and before she headed off to school. I could not help but to hope that I would not be there long enough for her to visit but thought that it would be fun to have a girls' weekend in the city.

Mark popped into the kitchen to grab a glass of water. He was glistening with a light sweat that he gets from working in the yard. This, mixed with the new sun, just made his tan that much deeper. After he downed a glass of water, he pulled his shirt off and grabbed another. I think he did it on purpose because he saw me staring again. Attraction had never been an issue for us. It was the timing and having time alone that was more of a problem. Just as it was right now. I had forgotten that Michele was still here until she cleared her throat and chuckled watching me stare at her father.

I turned to look at Michele, who now had a Cheshire cat grin. She crossed her arms and said "Oh, are you back?" and laughed.

I could feel my face turn six shades deep of red. I stammered, "I-I-I was just, ummm, I had not noticed that he came in, and it startled me, that's all."

Michele laughed. "Sure, Mom! Anyway, as I was saying, we can plan a long weekend and do some shopping at the outlets to get some school supplies and things to outfit my dorm. How does that sound?"

Before I had a chance to answer, Mark had walked over to the table where we were sitting. "Are you two planning a trip away?"

I looked up to speak, but Michele beat me to it. "Mom and I were just talking about having a weekend away at her place so I can see it and do some shopping."

And there it was. The look on Mark's face went from happy and curious, even mischievous, to hurt and withdrawn. "Oh, that's cool.

Sounds like fun. Well, I had better get back to it." With that, Mark went back out the door and into the yard.

I had been trying to circumvent that conversation because I knew it was just another twist of the knife in his back. Here in our house and around the familiar, it was easy to pretend that nothing had changed. Nothing other than sleeping arrangements anyway. But talking about my place or Portsmouth or anything new in my life was a reality check. A reality that he did not want and was still having a hard time dealing with.

Michele's phone rang, and when she looked at it, she smiled at me and headed up the stairs. From the sounds of it, she was going to be a little while, so I decided to wander outside to try to talk to Mark.

In the backyard, Mark was doing some yard cleanup like he had done hundreds of times before. It was a warm summer day, so he was glistening with sweat. The sight of him in the sun, shirtless and sweaty, stopped me in my tracks. I had no idea how long I stood there staring at him. He must have sensed someone was watching him because he stopped what he was doing, stood upright and stiff, and slowly turned around to look at me. I felt like a deer in the headlights being caught staring at him. I could not help myself, and I could not stop. I felt like a schoolgirl. My knees and legs were all wobbly, my mouth was hanging open, and I stared like an idiot. It was like I was seeing him for the first time.

Mark looked at me and just stared back with a slight smile. At first, neither of us said anything, and neither of us looked away. I could feel my cheeks getting hot, but I was not sure if it was embarrassment or excitement. I finally had to turn away. I tried to act as nonchalant as possible glancing around the yard, acting like I was looking at his work when all I kept seeing in my head was that body. The icebreaker was when I was not looking at where I was walking and tripped over the leaf blower. The resulting trip and fall was anything but graceful. I just sat there for a couple of minutes trying to massage my ego while Mark came running to my rescue.

"Are you okay?" Mark gushed.

I took one look at him and started laughing. When he realized I was laughing and not hurt, he joined in the laughter. I laughed far longer than I normally would have if the situation had not been so awkward.

Marked helped me to my feet and asked, "Are you sure you are not hurt?"

I answered, "No, I'm not hurt." *Just my pride after that awkward display.* I was not sure which was more embarrassing, not being able to stop staring at him or the fall. I just wanted out of the situation as fast as possible. "I was just coming to see what you were doing. Michele left me for a guy." I laughed.

"Oh, and here I thought you came to gawk like I was a Magic Mike show or something." Mark laughed.

I could feel the heat rising in my face again. "I wasn't gawking! I was…" But I could not finish my sentence. Mark started looking at me with those eyes and that smile of his. He was standing right next to me so I could see the sweaty muscles even better. His smell, a combination of musk and my favorite deodorant that he wore, was all around me. I had to look away and find something to focus on to clear my head.

I suddenly felt his hand on my leg, and I pulled away. "I'm sorry, I just noticed that you have a cut that is bleeding."

I looked down to see that I had actually cut myself in my fall. It was bleeding and running down my leg. "Oh, wow, I didn't even feel that. It isn't anything, just a little cut," I said trying to brush it off and thankful that I had something else to think about rather than him. I just needed him to move away from me so that I could not smell him anymore.

I stood up and headed toward the house to clean up my leg. Mark followed. In the kitchen, I was doing everything I could to avoid being near him or looking at him. I went about cleaning up my leg and trying to see if I needed a bandage. What was really going through my mind was the question of "what is wrong with me?" I have or had everything a woman could ever dream of, right here, in the palm of my hand. I had an incredibly sexy, devoted husband who truly loved me. I have amazing kids, a dream house, the career, everything. Yet I chose to walk away.

I was pulled out of my self-pity by Michele standing over me, hands on her hips. "I left for like two minutes and I come back to find you bleeding. What did you do?" She looked at Mark, and he just started laughing.

Mark started to explain. "I turned around, and there comes your mother, like a bull, down the walk, trips over the leaf blower, and did the worst gymnastics routine I have ever seen. As graceful as a monkey!" He belly-laughed at the memory of my falling.

I could not help but laugh. Michele looked at me, and I just shrugged. "What can I say? He's not wrong!"

Mark headed back outside, and Michele announced that she was going to run out to meet some friends. I told her it was fine as I really needed to think about packing up and making my trek back up north. I could not bring myself to say "home" as I really did not feel like that was home. I didn't even know where home was anymore.

I headed upstairs to pack my things and clean up the guest room after my goodbyes with Michele. As I was pulling the sheets off the bed, Mark came and stood in the doorway. "Michele told me you were getting ready to leave."

"Yeah, I need to start my trip back north since I have a bit of a ride. I need to get ready for the week."

"I wish you didn't have to go. It's been really nice having you back home."

I didn't even need to turn around to see the look on his face. I wanted to tell him that I loved being home, that I missed him, that I just wanted this situation over, but I couldn't. How do I do that? Instead I did not turn around and just said, "I know, me too."

I continued to clean up, and I knew he was standing there just watching me.

When I finally finished up and could no longer avoid looking at him, I turned toward the door. There were tears in his eyes when he looked at me and smiled.

"Then don't leave…again." He took a step toward me.

I froze and just looked back at him, now with tears in my eyes. "Mark, you know I have to. I have a place up there. I have a job. My life is up there now. Plus, I cannot do that to the kids. That is so confusing."

Mark looked me in the eye, took a step toward me, and said, "What about me? What about us, and what this is doing to us?"

I froze. After all that I had put him through, how could he not hate me? He would actually take me back.

"How would this even work? I left and broke this family. I don't even know what I want!" That was not a total lie. I believed that I knew what I wanted, but it didn't make sense since I had it and then walked away from it. I really felt like I needed to figure out what it was that I had been looking for before I jumped back to this. I could not hurt him again. There may not be a next time to fix it. I had to be sure before I made any sudden changes again.

"Mark, I have never stopped loving you, but I'm not ready for this." I walked past him and brought the sheets to the laundry room. I grabbed another set to remake the bed and headed back to the guest room, expecting to find him there when I returned. He was gone. I was more disappointed than I expected to be. I finished remaking the bed, packed up my things, and headed downstairs.

Mark was nowhere to be seen. I decided it would probably be easiest to not have a long goodbye scene, so I wrote a quick note, thanking him for the hospitality. I started to sign it like I always had but stopped. Then I wrote simply "L."

As I drove away, I had a terrible sinking feeling. This was not at all what I wanted. I did not want to be going "home" to a place where none of my family lived. It was new and exciting and different, but it was not at all home. I missed my kids, I missed my normal, and I missed Mark. Yet there was something that still pulled me away.

Returning back to the apartment was not at all as exciting as it had been the first few times I had done it. It was different, and it was my space, but now I did not see it as chic and modern. All I could see was lonely. I had no one to share my days with or dinner and talk about my day in the evening. It would be a lie to say that I did not enjoy only being responsible for myself instead of an entire household of people. That was exhausting and daunting and yet amazing knowing that I was responsible for keeping those people, my family, alive, healthy, and happy. Now, I was just responsible for keeping myself alive. As far as the happy goes, the jury was still out on that one!

The days turned into weeks, and the weeks into months. I was busy getting acclimated into my new position at the university. It was very different from being a practicing attorney. No deadlines or constant meetings or reviewing all the junior attorneys' work. The best part was leaving my job at the office when I was not there. Also, again not being financially responsible for all our employees. As a partner, that responsibility was on our shoulders, and while we were very successful and had built quite an empire, that was something that still kept me up at night. One bad case or bad decision and we could be on the streets looking for new jobs, and I would be out of my entire retirement plan. Not that leaving the firm and taking this position was not a major change in that plan, but honestly, for someone who has spent her entire life planning down to every minute detail, I had not given it any thought. I knew what I needed in order to survive, and I did it. In retrospect, I have to wonder if it was not a midlife crisis.

After being back at the house and spending time with Mark, I couldn't give a clear reason for leaving. I knew that I was not happy. I thought that we were not happy, but now I was questioning everything. Why was I not happy? I had everything that I had ever wanted. Did I want more? Did I want less? Did I want different? I had no idea. I just knew that now I was really not happy.

The only problem was that now that the wheels were set in motion, I had no idea how to brake without crashing.

Mark and I continued to communicate on a pretty regular basis. In fact, I could not remember a day that we had not texted one another or spoken on the phone. He texted me every morning to say good morning and to have a good day. At one point, I asked him why he never stopped this even after what I had done. He told me it was because nothing had changed for him. He still loves me, and he had said good morning and have a good day every day since we met. He said he also had no intention of stopping, so he hoped that my next husband didn't mind. I chuckled at that although the thought of that made my heart sink.

In all the years that we have been together, I have never once imagined myself without him, much less imagine myself with someone else. We have a friend who lost her husband very suddenly. She could not do anything for herself and had to rely on us to help her to learn everything from writing a check, to how to pay bills, and even learn to drive. Mark and I talked often about how either of us could be self-sufficient if we needed to be, but I cried every night for weeks thinking that I would not be able to mentally handle being without Mark.

When she became more stable and able to be more independent, she started to work and got on her own two feet. I saw her about nine months after his passing, and she had a new boyfriend. Later, as we lay in bed, I said to Mark, "I don't know how she could move on so quickly. I could never even imagine *ever* wanting to date someone else. I would rather be a lonely old spinster lady with twenty cats than to date anyone else."

He just looked at me and laughed and said, "I cannot see you with twenty cats."

I was serious about not being able to date again although probably not about the cats. I was not going to lie. I had noticed other men. Everyone notices other people. However, beyond the initial "Oh, he's cute" or "I like his smile," I didn't have any further interest. The perfect example was the cute guy in the coffee shop before I left for Michele's graduation. He was certainly attractive and interesting to talk to in that moment. However, I did not give him a second thought until now.

Mark sensed my hesitation after his comment about my next husband. "I'm sorry, I was just kidding. If I don't joke about this situation, I will go crazy missing you."

"Mark, how can you possibly still miss me or even want to still be with me after what I have done to you and our family? I don't want to be with me, and I'm stuck!"

Mark laughed and said, "Because I have always loved you. From the time I saw you walking across campus in your torn jeans, pink socks, and crazy flock of seagulls hair, I knew I only ever wanted to be with you. That has never changed just because our current living conditions have. I'm just hoping that you will fix whatever is going on with you and come back."

There it was. Now I remember why I left. If he did not understand something, it was ridiculous. For someone who was an engineer, to not understand something and just immediately think it was ridiculous was beyond me. I had to stop and decide whether I wanted to have the same fight that we had been having for years or if I just wanted to walk away from this one. I just did not know what kind of message that would send. If I let it slide, I am allowing him to think it's alright to dismiss my feelings. If I argue with him, it honestly gets us nowhere. Unfortunately, the spicy side of me won.

"Well, Mark, I see that our years of counseling and having the counselor that *you* picked tell you to stop dismissing my feelings has really sunken in for you. You continue to fail to understand that you do not have the right to dismiss how I feel about anything, whether you can understand it or whether you think it is ridiculous is completely irrelevant. Do you want to know exactly why I left? This... this, Mark, is why I left! Because you have made it abundantly clear over and over that I am irrelevant. I have to go, I will talk to you later." As I disconnected the phone, I could hear him say, "Laur—"

I had no interest in hearing what he had to say. I stood there staring at the wall. Part of me was so angry. Part of me was hurt that he still did not get it. Then there was a part of me that felt some sense of relief that I was validated for my leaving. It was not just a whim that I was now regretting. I had left for a reason; whether it was a very obvious reason or not, it was a reason. I am not irrelevant. My feelings were not irrelevant, and I will not continue to be treated like this every time he did not understand my feelings on something. I am entitled to my feelings. He did not need to like them, but he needed to respect that I felt a certain way.

With that, I grabbed my things and headed off to the coffee shop to start my day. As I walked at nearly a sprinter's pace because of my anger, I hardly noticed the man walking toward me until it was almost too late. I was quickly pulled from my self-pity when I heard "*Woah*, watch where you are going!"

I looked up to see "coffee shop guy" less than a foot in front of me trying hard not to dump his large steaming cup of something on himself or me. I took a quick sidestep to the right, nearly falling off the granite curb onto the cobblestone street but catching myself just before I made the entire situation worse by falling on my face. As I stood there taking a breath to figure out if I had hurt anything with that acrobatic move that I just made or whether I was wearing any of the scalding liquid from "coffee shop guy's" cup, I just burst into uncontrollable laughter. You know the kind of laughter when you are overly tired, in an awkward situation, or with your best friend and you feed off one another's laughing? That kind of laugh. It took a while for me to regain my composure all the while I had started to notice a small crowd gathering around us asking if I was alright.

"I am so sorry! I should have been watching where I was going." I was finally able to say through my tears from laughing so hard. "It's been a crappy morning all the way around, and if you can't laugh at yourself, what are you to do?" I tried my best at humor to cover up what an absolute idiot I felt like in this moment.

"I am fine. Are you sure that you are alright? That little dance step you did looked painful."

Well, at least "coffee shop guy" had a sense of humor! "Nice to see you again. Although this time was a bit more dramatic! Again, I am so sorry. I really should have been more careful."

"No apology necessary. I'm just glad that you did not get hurt! I almost burned you."

We stood awkwardly for a minute until I said, "Well, nice to see you again. I really have to run to get to work. I hope to see you again. Next time, I will see you before I almost run into you! Have a great day!"

"Thank you, you too! And be careful out there!" he called after me.

Well, if my day had not started bad enough, that just topped it. *Good thoughts, Laura. Let's just move past all this. Pack it in a box and get through this day!*

As I expected, I did not hear from Mark the rest of that day or the next. My mind was swimming, bouncing between being angry that he reminded me exactly why I had left, being grateful that he did remind me because I was starting to question my sanity in leaving everything that I had ever wanted, and being sad that in this situation, Mark still could not see what was wrong and try to fix things. He said that he missed me. Well, if he missed me enough to want to fix things, then he needed to make some changes!

By the end of the week, I had moved past the fight and was back to working on creating this new life of mine. I decided to join a gym just to get out of the condo and meet people and to take my mind off my misery. I also needed to work off some pent-up frustrations that were starting to rear their ugly heads now that I had been alone for so long.

It had become a regular thing to see my friend, John, at the coffee shop. We always chatted a bit over waiting to order or waiting for our orders. It never went beyond "How is your day going," "It looks like the weather may turn bad for the weekend," or other idle chitchat. But we always left with the promise of possibly having something more tomorrow. Tomorrow was just taking its time.

I was becoming a regular at the gym because, honestly, it was nice to be able to put on my headphones and just focus on what I was doing in that moment. It was the only time that I was really able to clear my head of all the other noise of work, the kids' lives, Mark, and just focus on me.

I knew it sounded like that was all I had been doing for the past several months, but that could not be further from the truth. The truth was that all I could think about was my family, my former life, that I had really made a mess of things. I could not stop thinking about Mark and that day in the yard or finding him coming out of the shower. I had seen that hundreds of times over the course of our years together, but I could not remember a single one of them. Why could I not remember them? That was pretty damned memorable, and yet try as I could, I was not able to remember. Now try as I could, I could not forget this one. Maybe it was the old adage that you always want something that you could not have.

I could have it; I just had to give up a lot to do so. Standing here now at the gym, trying to forget what I had lost and alone in my self-pity, I'm not sure that I would have been giving up much. I just could not bring myself to call him and ask him to take me back. Was it pride? Fear? Or just me being stubborn? Ironically, that was one of the arguments that Mark always had. He was constantly telling me that I was too stubborn for my own good sometimes. Of course, me being stubborn argued that was not the case at all, that I was just determined. I didn't think that determination was my reason here at all.

For the first time in my life, I had created a situation without thinking first, at least not really thinking long-term, and I was not able to control the outcome. The months of planning and fretting over whether I was doing the right thing by leaving, I had sworn I knew exactly what I wanted, and that this was the best thing for me and my family. Now all these months later, the family seemed to be moving on just fine. It was me that seemed to be stuck in the situation and in my own misery.

As I was wallowing in self-loathing on my treadmill with anger rock blasting in my ears, I could feel someone watching me. This was not an altogether unusual feeling. For anyone that had ever been to a box-store gym, they didn't call them meat lockers for nothing. It seems like 30–40 percent of the people here are actually trying to get fit, and 59–69 percent are trying to find a date. I was the 1 percent that was trying to escape life.

That uneasy feeling was growing, and reluctantly, I turned to see what was causing it. As I looked over, I was surprised to see coffee shop John standing next to me, pointing at my headphones. Apparently, I was not expecting that surprise because I tripped over my foot, nearly falling off my treadmill. John reached out, catching me before I hit the ground that would have certainly resulted in my being shot off the end of the treadmill for all the gym to gawk at and laugh at later in the locker rooms.

"Oh my god, thank you! You rescued me and my pride in one movement," I said as I tried to make light of my misstep.

"I'm so sorry that I startled you! I was trying to get your attention without scaring you but clearly did not do a very good job of it!" John said as he turned an odd shade of red for someone who always seemed so well put together and confident.

I could not decide if this uneasy shyness was cute and attractive or if it was a red flag that I should fake injury and bow out now. I decided to stick it out and see where this went.

"Well, you definitely have my attention now." I laughed. "Funny seeing you here and not at the coffee shop. It's always odd to see someone in a place different than where you are used to seeing them. I almost would not have recognized you without your business attire!"

"I was thinking the same thing about you! I almost didn't recognize you in yoga pants instead of dress pants and heels…not that I notice everything that you wear, that would be creepy." John laughed an uncomfortable laugh that started as a chuckle, but the more uncomfortable you get, the harder you laugh. "I am so sorry, that sounded so weird! It sounded so much better in my head!" As he was trying to make the situation less awkward, he was getting redder.

"John, it's fine." I laughed. "I get what you meant." Now it's my attempt at lightening the situation. "Although first the coffee shop, and now my gym? I have to wonder if you are stalking me!" I laughed, but the look on John's face was sheer panic. "Oh, I was really kidding!" I said, trying to make him stop looking at me like I was about to call the police.

Well, this entire situation certainly helped take my mind off my other issues, but now with this new issue, I was really ready to be out of this situation now. "Well, John, I don't mean to be rude, and please don't think it was because of this really odd exchange, but I really do need to get going. I have a bunch of work that I have to finish up tonight. I just wanted to let off some steam before jumping in. I hope to see you at the coffee shop this week! See you later," I called out as I headed toward the locker room.

As I walked away, I glanced back, noticing that John had looked around the room as if to make sure no one else had seen what just happened, then he turned back to watch me walk away. I gave him a quick wave and disappeared into the locker room to grab my things. I stayed a few minutes longer than necessary, really just waiting to make sure he had gone, then I headed out to door and to my car.

As I was driving home, I was thinking and laughing to myself about how awkward that entire simple exchange had turned. I had seen this guy several times over the past few months and had great brief discussions with him. This was certainly a side of him that I had not seen before, and I didn't think that I would want to see again.

I could not help but to compare John to Mark. I had never seen a side of Mark that I thought awkward or that made me uncomfortable. From the minute I saw him, I was completely enamored. I wanted to see more of him, get to know him more, and I did anything that I could just to catch a glimpse of him. I cannot imagine ever feeling that way about another man. I know that when I met Mark, I was very young, and young love is different from mature love, but I still couldn't stop comparing every man that I meet to Mark. I am going to be a very lonely lady if I don't get him out of my head or get this situation figured out!

Throughout our relationship, Mark and I had a knack for finishing each other's sentences, trying to call one another at the same time, starting a conversation that the other was just about to start with no prior premise, and just feeling like we were always on the same page. Distance did not seem to have stopped this oddity. Every time I am caught in thought about us or the past or wondering what he is doing now, he calls or I get a text from him. Some call it fate. I call it connection. We have had this connection from the moment we met. I was drawn to him in a way that I have never experienced before. It was as if he was new and exciting and yet old and familiar at the same time. The way I always described it, he was like home.

Finding a new "home" was proving to be extremely difficult when I still felt that intense draw to him. I was still calling or texting him when something exciting happened or when something really upset me. It seemed like the only thing that I did not talk to him about was us. I honestly did not know how to approach that subject.

Since the visit back for Michele's graduation, I had been reeling, and I couldn't seem to get my feet back on the ground. I was desperately trying to hold onto my new life and continue to build on that, but the draw of Mark and *our* life was overwhelming sometimes. I wanted to prove something to myself, but at this stage of it, I was not even sure what that was anymore. I knew that I could be independent. I knew that I was strong and successful and fully capable of being on my own. So what was I trying to prove?

When I talked to Mark, it was as if things had never changed and I'm just at work or out of the house. We talked about the kids and how they were or what we didn't agree with them doing. With the kids being grown, there really was no more talk about sports or schedules or who needed to pick which kid up from what event. Now it was more about the new things in our lives while trying to dance around the fact that we had separate lives. We were both painfully aware of that fact but tried hard not to mention it or make it obvious in our conversations.

There was also that playful, flirty banter that we had always shared. Before I left, that would have grown hotter and lead to retiring early. Now, it was brief and more veiled than it had been previously. It also always stopped just short of crossing any lines. That was an odd feeling as we were still married. There had been no discussion of formalizing any separation or divorce papers. It was going on five months since I had left, and we had not really moved forward with anything.

Then one day in late September, I had just come home from work and was on the phone talking to Jordyn about her new dorm room and how her classes were going. I was browsing through my mail while talking, and Jordyn asked me, "So did Dad tell you about his date?"

That question stopped me cold. I felt as if I had been hit with a truck that I never saw coming. I dropped my mail and my drink that I had been holding. As I stood there just staring at the phone, I was trying to figure out if this was a dream or if I had really just heard my daughter say that my husband had a date.

"Mom? Mom, are you okay? What happened?" was all I could hear Jordyn saying as I was trying to pull myself out of my shock.

"No, honey, I'm fine. Sorry, I just dropped my drink on the floor. So what do you mean your father has a date? I didn't know he was looking." I tried to sound nonchalant and not let the tears catch in my throat that were threatening to pour down my face. After all, I did not have a right to be upset. I made my bed! I left and started a new life. leaving him holding down the house, the kids, and our family while I went off to find myself.

"It was really kind of my fault. Well, Michele's and my fault. We were having coffee at the house with him a couple of weeks ago, and he was looking really sad, so Michele said that he should get out. I said that I had seen this dating site that is not like a hookup site and that he should try. He was really not interested at first, but we thought it would be good to get him out so he stopped moping around so much. We helped him set it up, and he got a few matches. Well, really more than a few. Like a lot more than a few."

"*Oh*! Well, I'm not surprised. Your father is a catch! I guess I'm just kind of surprised that he went along with it. It doesn't seem like his style." I fought hard to try not to sound upset or jealous. I didn't want her to feel bad that she had told me anything. I was also still stuck on the fact that he was sad and moping around the house. Part of me was really happy to hear that he missed me.

"It definitely was not his style. We have had to coach him about what to say and how not to sound like too much of a geek!" Jordyn laughed. "But he seemed to connect with some nice ladies. He is trying to set up a time for a coffee date. I think they are going sometime this weekend."

"Really? So soon? Well, good for him. We would not want him to keep moping around over me, would we?" I tried to make a joke of it, but it came out sounding harsher and pettier than I had planned.

"Well, Mom, you did leave him, so what did you expect he would do? You are out playing, and he should sit home waiting for an *if*? That's not exactly fair!" Jordyn spat back.

"Woah, first of all, I don't like your tone! I am still your mother, so have some respect. Second, I was trying to make a joke although poorly. And third, I am not 'out playing.' As a matter of fact, other than work, the gym, and the coffee shop for my morning coffee, I am barely leaving the house. However, what happens or happened between your father and I is really between us. That being said, I am happy for him if this is what he wants and what will make him happy. Just do me a favor, please don't tell me anything more." I was struggling between wanting to know more and not wanting to hear it. I was still reeling at the idea of Mark giving other women a second thought, much less going on a date. That stung more than I wanted to admit.

"I am sorry, Mom, I probably should not have told you. You are right. Well, I need to run because I have to get ready for my next class. I will talk to you later this week?

"Of course! Have a good class. Talk to you later, love you!" As I hung up the phone, I resisted the urge to call Mark to ask him about his date and his newfound popularity among the ladies.

Mark had always been extremely popular. I could see the looks he got and the whispers about him when we went to functions or parties, even out with our friends. He was very good-looking, well-built, and extremely outgoing and personable. This, in conjunction with his new freedom, was a recipe for disaster if I had any type of hope for a reconciliation. What if he found someone that was better suited or he found someone he was extremely attracted to? I had not thought about those possibilities before, and this was scaring the hell out of me. What had I done?

I spent the rest of the afternoon in a daze going through the worst-case scenarios in my head and envisioning him at his computer or on his phone chatting with one woman after another. Worse, what those women were saying to him or what pictures they might be sending. In today's society, it is so easy for people to exchange the raciest photos. Women think nothing of exposing and photographing any part of their body that they think will get them a man. That was my competition now. Congratulations, Laura, you have gone too far!

My only hope was the fact that we were still married and we had not had any discussions about ending that! Not yet at least.

I decided that my overthinking was not doing me any good, so I just turn on one of my old favorite movies and try to clear my head. I changed into my comfy PJ's, grabbed my glass of wine, and headed to my room to relax. As I was getting comfortable, I got a text. It was Mark asking if I was busy. I hesitated to answer. I was not sure that I was ready to talk to him yet after just having received this information.

I texted back that I was just crawling into bed to watch a movie but I was not too busy. Then he asked if he could call. That was the first time that he has asked before calling me. That could not be a good sign. I answered back with "Of course, you can!"

As my phone rang, it took every ounce of my being to answer it. When I did, I was trying to sound as normal as possible. "Hey, what's up?" I answered.

"Hey, umm…I just wanted to talk quick. I'm not interrupting anything, am I?" Mark asked, sounding like something was wrong but not bad, just making him uncomfortable.

I tried to ease the conversation by saying "Well, after a crappy day, you are interrupting my glass of Pinot Grigio and a good chick flick, so out with it." I chuckled as I said it even though I was feeling anything but jovial.

"So I have an awkward situation," Mark started as if he had not heard my joke at all. "I'm not sure how to approach it, and now I'm probably overthinking it, so I need to talk it through."

"Okay, now you are making me feel uncomfortable. I cannot remember the last time you overthought anything. I will help you if I can. What's the situation?" I asked. Although now I was wondering if this so-called situation was his date, and if it was, I did not want to know anything more than I already do!

"Man, I am not even sure how to talk to you about this. Maybe this was a mistake. I may want to think about this a little more. I'm sorry, it's just too weird." Mark was stuttering and really acting uncomfortable. I didn't think I had ever seen him act like this. Now I really did not want to know what he was going to ask me.

You know that feeling when you are being called to the principal's office or your boss's office and you know that you are not going to like what is about to happen? The anticipation is so much worse than the actual thing that is about to happen. Your stomach does flip-flops. Your palms get sweaty. You can feel your heart beating in your head. That is the feeling that I had right now. I knew what was coming, and I really did not want to have this discussion because having the discussion meant that I had to face reality. A reality that I had caused in a domino effect of my life literally falling down around me. I didn't know how I could have ever thought that I could walk away from things to go off and create my new life and expect that my old life would not change. Like it would just wait there for me as if I had just run off to do errands.

As I sat there wondering how I could have allowed this fracturing of my beautiful universe to get this far without hitting the reverse button, I could not help but to think that I would never recover from this moment. Mark continued to stumble over his words on the other end of the phone, starting and stopping his sentence a dozen times. Finally, that anticipation got the better of me, and I blurted out, "Mark, I know about the dating sites!" As soon as the words were out of my mouth, I wished that I could take them back.

"What do you mean you know? How? Oh no, don't tell me that the girls told you!" I could hear the wheels turning in his head, and I instantly felt bad that I had outed Jordyn.

"Was that what you were trying to tell me?" I asked, trying to change the subject. "If so, you don't need to be so uncomfortable telling me." I was trying hard to sound convincing, but I was not even convincing myself that I was okay with all this because honestly, I was not!

"So you are okay with my dating?" Mark asked, sounding almost hurt.

"Well, I mean, if that is what you want to do, I cannot tell you no. I can't exactly expect you to wait around pining over me forever, right?" Or could I? I was the one that left, and I was pining over him. It was at this moment that I could not explain why I had not gone home. I didn't know what was keeping me here. I could have returned to my old job in a heartbeat. Breaking my lease would have been easy enough. Still there was something that was keeping me from making the choice to go home. Was it pride? Fear of rejection? I could not say.

There was a long pause on the other end of the line. "Hello?" I asked. "Are you still there, or did I lose you?"

"No, I'm still here. Sorry, I am really distracted tonight. I must just be tired," Mark said although not very convincingly.

"So is that all you wanted to talk about? You actually have not even told me what you were going to say. I kind of stole your thunder."

"I just mainly wanted to tell you about the site. I didn't want you to hear it from anyone else and be blindsided, but apparently, I was too late."

"So how is that going? Or is that too personal?" I asked cautiously. I did not actually want to know if he was going to be seeing someone, but the not knowing was even harder. Part of me was hoping that he would tell me it was a big mistake and he never should have done it. But that was the selfish part of me who was also very relieved to find out he was moping around the house after me.

"I don't know," Mark answered. "It is just weird. Nothing at all like meeting someone back in the day. Everyone has an angle. I don't know if someone is real or a catfish."

I laughed. "No, Mark, that is you don't know if you are being catfished. Someone is not a catfish."

"See? I don't even know the lingo! I am a complete disaster at all of this. And to be honest, I do not want to be doing any of it. I just want to be back to us. There! I said it. I want to wake up from this whole nightmare and find you next to me and our life back to normal. Nothing is normal, and I hate it!" I could hear the catch in his throat when his voice trailed off.

It took me a couple of minutes to respond because I did not want him to hear that I was crying. Why? I didn't know. "I am sorry, Mark. I'm sorry that I have hurt you. I'm sorry that I just left. I am sorry that I have made such a mess of things. I just don't know what to say or do at this point."

After a short silence from Mark, he said, "Neither do I, Laura. I will talk to you later. Bye!" Then he hung up the phone.

This was not at all how I expected this conversation to go. I was trying to tell him that I did not know how to fix it. This was not one of those situations that I could just take over and fix myself. I had really made a mess of things, and I did not know how to fix it. I was trying to ask for help, but I don't think that was how he took what I said. Now I was left holding the phone, wishing I could explain what I was trying to say and realizing that I may have just pushed him away for the last time.

Should I call him back? Should I text and explain that he took what I said the wrong way? As I was trying to decide what to do, my phone rang. It was Daniel calling for our weekly catch-up. Mark would have to wait a little longer. I just hoped that he would still be there.

The next morning, I was still trying to figure out how to handle the situation with Mark. I was on my way to work, stopping for my morning coffee, and bumped right into John.

He looked at me and laughed. "We really need to stop meeting like this. People are going to start to talk!"

"Oh my gosh, I am so sorry! I am really distracted this morning and was not watching where I was going…again!" I was so embarrassed, and I could feel the blood flooding to my face. I hated that I had such a telltale face for every emotion!

"I don't mind at all. I rather like bumping into you. I would like to do it more in fact."

The inflection in John's voice made me jerk my head to see if the facial expression matched his tone. Yes, it certainly did. I do believe this is what is called flirting. It had been so long since someone had flirted with me that I had no idea what it looked like anymore. It took me by such surprise that I stood staring at him like to complete idiot. I had no idea what to say.

"I am so sorry! I hope I didn't make you uncomfortable. I was just kidding. Oh, jeez, now I feel like a fool. Please forgive me. I will just…ummm…okay, well it was nice to see you." With that, John was off.

I was not exactly sure what had just happened. Maybe I read more into that exchange. Maybe he was not actually flirting. I have no idea what happened to my brain either! Why would words not come out of my mouth? I knew it had been a while since anyone had tried flirting with me, but I just froze!

If Mark is as bad at this as I appear to be, maybe I will not have any reason to be worried.

Several days went by with no word from Mark. It was not really normal to have no communication at all from him even if it was just about something with the house or mail or one of the kids. I had started to text him several times, but it all seemed ridiculous, like I was trying to find something to talk to him about. In all honesty, I was. I missed him terribly. Our daily communication had become such second nature that I missed it. But again, how could I expect that to continue? I left. I have to keep reminding myself that I made the conscious decision to walk away from everything in my life. I had no right to expect anything or anyone to try to return or stay in my life. If I wanted to make someone stay or go back to what I had, I was the one that was going to have to make the move to make that happen. I could not expect anyone to come to me.

I replayed in my head over and over what I was going to say to Mark. How do I approach it? Just jumping right into "Hey, I'm an idiot, so I'm coming home. Let's just forget this all happened" seemed a little outrageous. Plus, I was not sure how this would play out or what I even wanted to happen. I knew that I wanted to keep Mark in my life, but in what capacity? Would he even want me back? Would we be able to move past this last year? These were all things that I needed to consider and expect the worst.

I decided that I needed to start to make the effort to have a discussion before it was too late and he found someone that he was interested in. That night, after I had cleaned up from dinner and I was finally able to sit down and put some thought into my message to him, I started my text.

"Hey, when you have a few minutes, I would really like to talk to you. The way we left things the other night was kind of awkward and not at all like how we normally communicate." No, I was not happy with that. So I started over.

"Hey, I don't like the way we left things the other night. I would really like to talk if you get a minute and would not mind talking to me." That was not great either, but I could not keep putting this off. The longer that I wait to try to talk to him, the more of a chance that I will lose him. So I hit send.

There is nothing longer than waiting for someone to respond to you when you are already on edge. I had to put my phone down because the anticipation was terrifying. Everything was going through my head, like what if he doesn't want to talk? What if he was on a date? What if he ignores my text? Do I send another? How long is long enough to wait to try again? What if he tells me that it is too late for us?

I got up, put my clothes together for the next day, pulled out a book to read, and tried to settle in, pretending that my phone was not sitting next to me doing nothing. There was no response text, no call, just silence. I checked my phone to make sure that the ringer was on. Then I thought that maybe I should text one of the kids just to make sure that I had service. I didn't know why I would not have service, but that was an explanation as to why he was not responding.

Eventually, I fell asleep waiting for the response that did not come.

They say that everything will look better in the morning. Well, those people clearly have not waited all night for a response to anything, and they have definitely not been an overthinker. After waking up and looking at my phone to see if I missed a call or text from Mark no less than fifteen times, I assumed the worst. He was in an accident or he was out on a date or even worse than those…he had stayed over another woman's house.

I went through every possible scenario in my head as to why he would not have at least sent me a text saying that he was not available to talk or we will have to talk later. Just something that would tell me he saw it! As I lay in bed scrolling through Facebook looking for evidence that he was out on a date or that he was somewhere that would explain the radio silence on his end, I was also contemplating whether I should text him again. Then I thought, well, if he is with someone, do I really want to do that? That led me to think that I might just want to do that with something like "Hey, it's just your WIFE! Where are you?" Then if he is lying next to someone else, they will see it, and it will ruin things for him. Of course, if he is not with someone else, that is just awkward.

I also contemplated contacting one of the kids, but I did not want to unnecessarily worry them or have them question why I needed to contact him so badly. The entire situation was giving me a headache. I really just needed to walk away from my phone and this debacle and try to refocus.

As I was making myself my first cup of coffee and watching the city start to awaken out my window, I heard the notification on my phone. My heart jumped, and I started to shake. I didn't even want to look at the phone for fear that I may not like what I saw. Instead, I played nonchalant, pretending like I didn't hear it go off. I didn't know who I was trying to fool because my brain was racing, and it was having a huge argument with my eyes that were doing everything that they could to avoid looking at the phone. Finally, my brain won out, and I had to look.

The universe has a very strange sense of humor because it was just an ad for a sale at the local grocery store. Okay, well that still left the question of where the hell was Mark and why he was not answering me. My fear and overthinking started turning to anger that he was not responding. He had no idea what I wanted to talk about! What if there was something happening with the kids or even with me?

Unless he saw the message and just flat-out ignored me, which was just as annoying because it was me! Not some floozy he had just met on the internet. We have a very long history, children, a home, and marriage papers together. He had to answer me!

Or maybe that was the reason. I was able to just up and move out leaving all of it, including him behind. This could be his way of making me feel what he had felt. Well, it was not exactly the same, but I could imagine that feeling of not knowing or just feeling lost and alone. That had to be the same.

As I drank my coffee, staring out the window at the city and the people just going about their day, I started to think how strange I felt in this place. I wanted to belong, and I live here, work here, shop here, and go to the gym here, but I didn't feel like I'm really part of any of it. I was going through the motions of doing what I needed to do to survive. I was very lonely. It was the first time in years that I had been alone for so long with no one to share my day with or even a meal. Sure, I talked to Mark pretty much daily, but I didn't tell him a lot that was happening because I felt like I was rubbing it in his face that I was part of a different world. It just did not feel right. Plus, he did not know anyone here or even my job for that matter. We trod very lightly when we talked about our living arrangements, my job, or anything about our locations.

It was ironic in a way. I left because I didn't think I was happy. I felt like things were stagnant. I wanted to be noticed, to be wanted, not just needed for the day-to-day. I wanted to be noticed as a person and as a woman. I wanted the companionship that I felt like I had lost with the hustle and bustle of our daily lives, the kids, our jobs, the house, and just life in general. When I asked to spend time doing things, he was always too busy or there was something else that needed to be done. The answer was always next weekend or maybe one night this week. Days turned to weeks, that turned to months, and before we knew it, the kids were almost all grown and just about out the door. The irony was that not only was that the time that we should actually have more time to be together and do things, but I left, and now I was completely alone. Now, I was definitely not happy. To make matters worse, the life that I was escaping from was crumbling.

While I was wallowing in my self-pity over my coffee, I received a notification. Out of pure habit, I looked at it. This time it was Mark. I paused for a minute to gather myself, and I picked up the phone.

The message read "Sure, call when you can." Seriously? You made me wait all night for a response, and that was all I got? No "Sorry, my phone died" or "Oh no, just seeing this now." Nothing but "sure." Well, now I was not sure that I wanted to talk. Maybe I will just give him a taste of what he gave me. Although with that message, I'm not sure it would have the same effect. He didn't seem too bothered by the fact that he was answering almost twelve hours later!

I threw the phone on the side table in the living room and headed toward the bedroom to get dressed for the day. Now I was irritated and wanted some retail therapy!

After I got dressed, I grabbed my purse and phone and started to head out the door. As I was putting my phone into my bag, I noticed another text and a missed call. Both were from Mark. I must have missed them when I was dressing in the other room.

This time, the text read "I'm sorry, I am just really waking up and read your message along with my response. I'm sorry that I didn't see it sooner. I know you, and you probably had me dead in a ditch somewhere. I didn't get you when I called, so I'm not sure if you are mad at me or just not able to grab the phone. Either way, call me when you get a minute so that we can talk."

Well, he was half right. I was overthinking but less of his bodily harm and more of something else with his body. I needed to give myself a few to stop feeling like I was crazy for thinking that he could have been with another woman and to allow myself to be able to speak to him without saying something stupid. I needed to assume that he had just fallen asleep or his phone died and he didn't see the message until this morning. Those were logical assumptions.

I still went out to go shopping. I needed to take my mind off this entire thing and be able to go back to it with a fresh perspective. As I walked toward the coffee shop, I was trying to think of how to word a response to him that did not sound as awkward as I felt. I finally decided on "Hey, out doing a bit of shopping. I should not be long, so I will call you when I get back." It was simple and did not sound crazy.

Walking through the shops, trying to refocus and figure out what I was going to say to Mark, without sounding like I should be committed, I started to question why I had been so upset. I'm not even sure that I have any right to be upset that he could have been with another woman. I left. But we were still married. I took those vows seriously. At one time, I thought he did as well. With the new information from Jordyn, I was questioning that. I understand that I had left and moved three states away six months ago. That did not change the fact that we were married. We had not discussed a divorce. We had not filed. I think I had the right to be upset that he was trying to date other people. That had not even really crossed my mind. I didn't understand how it crossed his.

I was not getting anywhere with my shopping since I hardly noticed anything that I was looking at in any of the stores. Since I was right near my coffee shop and I had missed breakfast and lunch, I decided to stop in for a quick cup, hoping that it will clear my mind. As I stood in line staring blankly at the menu that I now knew by heart and waiting for my turn, I heard a familiar voice behind me.

"It's a little late for your morning coffee!" I didn't even need to turn around to know that it was John.

"I could say the same about you!" I said as I turned to face him. He was dressed in a jogging suit and looked like he had run in from the other side of town. "Well, you are not really dressed the way I am used to seeing you either! Can I assume you actually took the weekend off?" I chided him.

"That I did." He laughed back. "I am not sure if you took it off or if you popped into the office today from your appearance. Beautiful as always."

I stared back at him, not quite knowing what to say. I cannot remember the last time a man, other than my husband or father, had told me that I looked beautiful. It felt a little strange. It must have been written on my face because he then looked at me and said, "I'm sorry, I hope I didn't offend you."

I snapped to and said, "Of course, you did not offend me! Being told I look beautiful is never offensive. I'm sorry, I just don't hear that very often, so it caught me off guard. And thank you, I feel anything but beautiful today. It's been a rough start."

"Well, I hope it is getting better now." John smiled. "Perhaps I can help make it even better!"

"Ummm, well...what did you have in mind?" I asked.

"Well, what are you doing this evening? I don't have anything planned, and I hear that O'Brien's Pub down the street is having a live band that sounded like it might be fun. It does not have to be a date, but it might be nice to go out somewhere other than meeting here all the time," John said as he looked around at the coffee shop.

"I don't know. I'm not sure I would be too much fun," I started to answer.

"Like I said, it does not need to be a date. I just get really tired of going home every night to an empty apartment and staring at my refrigerator that has not learned how to cook yet. It would be nice to just get out of there for one evening and actually talk to another adult. What do you say? Save me from my sad life? Even just for one night?"

As much as I felt like I probably should not, I could not help but to say yes. "Sure, I could use some time out of my place too. Plus, I have not grabbed groceries and don't have much to cook. But you may be sorry about the adult conversation once I start talking!" I tried to make light of it, but I was not sure that I would be able to stop the word lava flow that I felt building up in my head.

"Perfect! Sounds like we could both use a night out! I will meet you here around seven, and we can walk to O'Brien's. That way you don't feel like it's a date. No pressures at all!" John said with a smile and a bow.

"I will meet you here at seven. Thank you! This may be just what I need to fix my crappy day!" I said, really meaning it.

"Any time," John threw back over his shoulder as he headed out the door and down the street.

I took a few minutes to sit in front of the coffee shop in the square and watch the people passing by. I had always loved people watching. Mark thought it was creepy, but I liked to try to guess what their story was. I would point out couples and say "They were high school sweethearts" or "Those two just met on Tinder, and they are just getting to realize that they have nothing in common."

Watching the families with their small children was my favorite. As a parent, you are so in the moment of how to handle every situation that you don't pay attention to the details of that moment. I loved watching the expression on children's faces as they interact with their parents or when they are seeing something new for the first time. The awe and wonder of being in a city and the hustle and bustle of it all. I remember how it made me feel the first time I was exposed to it, and then being able to see it in a child's face was just the best.

I slowly made my way back to my apartment after my people-watching therapy, sipping my coffee on the bench in the square. It seemed somehow better than feeding pigeons in the park, but I'm not sure how. I was laughing to myself at what I had become and what I did for fun now when my phone rang.

After digging around for it in my purse, I grabbed it without looking at who was calling. "Hello?"

"Jesus, Laura, I was starting to get worried. I thought you said you were going shopping! It has been hours, and I have not heard a word. Did you not see any of my texts, or are you ignoring them?" Mark was angrier than I had heard him in a long time.

I glanced at my phone and saw the fourteen text messages from him and a few from the kids. I would have to remember to respond to them right after this situation.

"I'm sorry, I just lost track of time. Wait…no, I am not sorry. I was out having a day to myself. At least you knew where I was! I did not hear a word from you all night. I had no idea where you were… or who you were with! So don't lecture me about my whereabouts." As soon as it came out of my mouth, I knew that I was in for a fight. I had not meant to say it. My defenses went into overdrive, and it just came out. There was that word lava I was talking about.

After a few minutes of silence that had me looking at my phone to make sure the call had not dropped, Mark quietly responded with, "What do you mean you did not know *who* I was with? What would ever make you think that I would be with anyone else?"

"Well, Mark, I could not get a response from you after texting you early in the evening. You did not respond until the next day, and all of this after learning that you had joined a dating site and were trying to have coffee dates with other women. Why do you think that I would say that?" I was not wrong in any of that. Although the coffee date comment kind of hit home. Wasn't that what I was doing with John? I had not gone out seeking him or joined a dating site. We had bumped into either other by happenstance and just happened to see each other almost daily because we go to the same coffee shop, so no, it is nothing like his situation.

"Wow! Is that what you think of me now? That since you just walked out of our lives, I just jumped right back into the saddle and started finding myself a new wife? Damn, Laura, I would have thought you knew me better than that!"

"Believe me, so did I, but I never expected you to run right out and join a dating site. You have never been one for peer pressure, so saying 'the girls talked me into it' is not a defense either!" I was trying not to sound as angry and bitter as I felt, but I could hear it in my voice. So could Mark.

"Well, *Laura*, I was left here holding things together while you went off to play in the city in your new life. I have no idea what you are doing there. For all I know, you have a different boyfriend for each night. So excuse me if I just wanted some companionship since my best friend decided to up and bail on our life together!"

And with that, the phone went dead. I looked at it several times to make sure. Mark had never hung up on me before. He did not believe in it. He said it was rude and disrespectful. This was after I did it to him a few times in our early years of dating. It made me feel so bad that I never did it again.

Now here I was holding the dead phone and thinking that he was rude and disrespectful but that I had handled that discussion all wrong. I didn't know what made me just throw all that at him right now. Maybe it was because he put me right on the defensive coming at me like he was my father and I was late for curfew. Whatever the cause, it was out there in the universe now, and I had no idea where we stood with things. I did know that it felt like we were getting farther and farther from where we were, and I had no idea how to get back.

I walked back to the apartment and headed upstairs. I kept checking my phone to make sure the sound was on in case he tried to call me again or texted an apology. So far, nothing. I responded to the kids' messages as if nothing had happened and my world was still normal. At least normal for my current state.

I paced around the apartment, acting like I was cleaning up when there was nothing to clean. I was barely ever at home, so everything was exactly the same as when I put it in its place months before. I had not turned on music like I normally did for fear of missing Mark's text or call. Yet I still checked my phone repeatedly. I finally decided to put on some smooth jazz just to calm my nerves and help distract me from the phone and my thoughts. Singing along, I started to calm down and even thought about what I would cook for dinner.

Oh my god, *dinner*! I had completely forgotten that I was supposed to meet John for dinner at seven. It was already after six, and I was not showered or close to being able to get out the door in time to meet him.

I quickly texted him that I was really running late and that if he wanted to cancel, I would completely understand. More importantly, I hoped he would cancel.

A response came back almost immediately that he was happy to make it later as he was also running a bit late and now he could get ready without rushing. Well, great! Now I had to go out on a pseudo-date after having an enormous fight with my husband about how I was not dating. The irony was not lost on me about this entire ridiculous situation or the fact that I was the root cause of all of it.

I half-heartedly prepared myself for my non-date date. I could not decide if I wanted to go all out and look good or if I wanted to just be natural. I wanted to prove, mostly to myself, that this was not a date and I was not really thinking like that. I decided that I wanted to get pretty for me, not because I was trying to impress anyone. I had been feeling very down lately and needed a little pick-me-up of sorts. Shopping was always my go to, but because someone had ruined that for me earlier, this will be the next best thing.

John was right, I did need to just get out and stop feeling sorry for myself. Everyone else was still living their life as if nothing had changed. My entire life had been turned upside down, but I needed to make the most of that and start living again.

I headed out the door and down to the evening city life. It was bustling with activity that was immensely different from the earlier activity of families and sightseeing. This was the life of the young and beautiful people getting out of their apartments and enjoying each other. We older folks usually missed this while watching our old movies and going to bed at sunset.

I was actually getting excited about being out and meeting John and having a conversation with someone who knew nothing of my past or present situation. Someone who just wanted to enjoy my company. I decided that the best way to fully enjoy the evening was to shut off my phone, so I did. Then I dropped it into my handbag and forgot about it the rest of the evening.

After meeting John for drinks, we decided to go to a quieter spot to eat so that we could talk without sounding like we were in a nursing home asking each other to repeat ourselves. I had forgotten how loud bars were. It had been years since Mark and I had done the nightlife. Okay, I need to stop referencing everything with "Mark and I." Even my thoughts were invaded by us.

We talked about everything from jobs, to living in the city, to dating in today's world with all the apps, and how people have no fear to say what they want behind a keyboard. John joked that "Back in our day, if you wanted to meet someone, you just said 'Hi, I'm John. What are you doing later?'"

I laughed. "Oh, so you mean like you did to me today?"

"Well, I guess you are right! Maybe things are not so different today!" We both laughed and chided about how the rest of the people in the restaurant had probably met through social media and not how we had.

Then the dreaded question… "So, Laura, what brought you to the city? I know you did not grow up around here because I did and you are definitely different. I'm guessing you are probably from the Connecticut area. Am I close?"

I paused, trying to figure out how to answer the question without going into all the sordid details of my failed marriage that I am not free of and explaining Mark and the kids. Not to mention my career as a successful lawyer turned recruiter.

"Oh, I'm sorry! That was very presumptuous of me." John looked around as if to make sure that no one else could hear him.

"You are not in the witness protection program, right?" He flipped his head around again, looking for anything unusual. "Your secret is safe with me…Laura." John emphasized my name and winked as he said it.

I could not help but to laugh. This was just the out I needed. I looked around and whispered, "Shhhhh…not so loud! If they hear you, I will have to get another new name and move again!" Then I laughed. It felt good and strange at the same time. I could not remember the last time that a man, other than Mark, had made me laugh like this. That was the one thing that Mark always said to me. "Well, if nothing else, I make you laugh!" And that he most certainly did!

John dropped the subject of my past, and I did not offer much more information. I told him that he was right. That I had moved from Connecticut. I told him that I had needed a change and got a job offer that intrigued me. Plus, I always wanted to live near an amazing coffee shop that I could walk to and hoped to someday meet friends that would hang out with me there. Then we both laughed at the reference, knowing that we were probably the only one's there that would get it.

After several hours, we both started to yawn. I looked at his phone on the table and could not believe it was after midnight.

"I never stay up this late unless there is a good movie marathon on!" I said as I was trying to stifle another yawn.

"Neither do I, but mostly because then I would just skip the gym in the morning and end up fat along with being old and boring!" John chuckled.

"I highly doubt that you would get fat, and if you are old, I am right there with you. But I definitely have you beat on boring! I almost canceled tonight because I was comfortable and did not want to have to get dressed again!" I confessed.

"Well, while we are confessing things, when I saw your text, I was almost hoping that you were canceling because I didn't want to go back out either. But I am really glad that you did not! I have enjoyed you and tonight. So thank you!"

I could feel myself blushing a little. "I am glad that I did not as well! I had forgotten how much fun the nightlife can be! Plus, I have really enjoyed having a conversation with someone other than my doorman or the students that I coach."

"So what do you say to doing this again sometime? But not too soon because going out too often may be too much of a shock to my system. I am old, don't forget!" John laughed.

"I would really like that. But we definitely have to give my system time to adjust." Part of me was intrigued by the thought of another night out with John. He was funny, smart, a great conversationalist, had so many of the same interests that I had, and I thoroughly enjoyed his company. The night had flown by just talking about nothing and everything. The other part of me could not help but to feel guilty like I was doing something wrong. I was still married although there was nothing wrong with a night out with a friend just to talk.

We left the restaurant and started to head down the street. Due to the late hour and my body not being accustomed to being out that late, I was a bit wobbly. It could have also been the few glasses of wine that I had consumed over the last few hours. John held his arm out for me to hold onto. I hooked my arm into his, and we walked along the street continuing to chat. *This is all very platonic*, I kept telling myself.

John walked me back to the area of the coffee shop and asked me which way to my apartment. I started to argue that he did not need to walk me all the way back. John insisted, explaining that due to the late hour and my unsteadiness, I would be an unsuspecting target, and he did not want to feel responsible if something were to happen to me. I reluctantly agreed although it was nice to have a knight in shining armor looking out for me.

When we reached my building, I turned to John and thanked him for walking me that far. "Are you sure you are ok to go upstairs?" John asked.

"I am fine, thank you. I really had a good time tonight. It was nice to get out and feel alive again! I am very glad that you suggested it. I hope to see you at the coffee shop soon?"

"Absolutely! I am there every morning. I had a great time as well. I am happy that you did not cancel. Maybe we can plan it again soon, but not too soon!" John laughed. He took my hand and kissed it then said good night and turned to walk home.

I stood there for a second then headed into the building. As I headed up in the elevator, I smiled thinking back on the evening. I had a much better time than I had anticipated. I didn't know why I was so apprehensive about going out.

When I got inside, I took my phone out and turned it back on. While I poured myself a glass of water, the messages started pouring in. I had twelve voicemail messages between Mark and the kids and over thirty text messages. Apparently, because I didn't answer my phone, everyone thought I was dead. My initial instinct was to apologize and try to smooth things over so no one was upset. Then I stopped and realized, *I am a damn adult*. I appreciated everyone's concern, but I was entitled to unplugging now and again without the need to explain myself to anyone! Years ago, we did not have cell phones! When I went out to do errands, no one could get in touch with me until I got home and either answered the phone or I returned a voicemail message.

While I was wallowing in my irritation, my phone rang, startling me from my thoughts. Instinctively, I grabbed and answered, "Hello?" Instantly, I regretted not screening my calls.

"Jesus, Laura, where the hell have you been? We have been trying to get you for hours!" Mark sounded partially irritated and partly panicked.

"Sorry, I was out, and it must have died in my purse." A little lie, but I did not want to have the conversation of how I was out with another guy with Mark right now even if it was platonic. "What is going on? I turned my phone back on, and I have a dozen or more missed calls and texts. You would have thought I had been off the grid for weeks!" I joked, trying to make things lighter. This was already ruining what had been a nice evening.

"Laura, there was an accident. Don't panic. Everyone is okay, but we are still at the hospital."

Instantly, my heart sank, and I felt like I was going to throw up. I had to sit down because my legs got weak and wobbly. "What do you mean…accident?" I was able to squeak out. "Who? How? When? What happened?" I asked.

The feeling of guilt for not answering or being near my phone became overwhelming, and I started to hyperventilate. I was trying not to let Mark hear me because I did not want him to ask any more questions. I had already started the conversation with a lie, I did not want to elaborate on it. After all, that was a minimal lie as my phone was off, just voluntarily.

"The girls and I decided to go to a movie, so we met up, and we were heading to the theater. We came to the light at the center of town. When we started to go, a car came out of nowhere and hit us broadside. Thankfully, they were not going too fast, but they were drunk. It pushed us through the intersection and into the pole on the corner. It took a while to get us out, but we are all alive. The other driver was fine, just a few bumps and bruises. Our car, on the other hand, was totaled."

"Totaled?" I said, still in shock. "They had to be going pretty fast for them to push your car that far and total it. The girls, are they okay? Who was on the passenger side?" I could barely breathe.

"Jordyn was on that side. She took the brunt of the impact. Thankfully, she saw it right before the impact and slid towards my side as much as she could. It could have been much worse. She has a concussion, broken right arm, and they have her in x-ray now for a possible pelvic fracture. Her arm may need surgery as it was broken in several places around her elbow. Otherwise, she is awake and talking. She's pretty angry that the EMTs had to cut her favorite sweater off of her, yelling that they were going to have to get her mother to buy her another one since that was why it was so special."

I laughed then cried. I cried so hard I could not hold the phone up anymore, and I could not catch my breath. I could hear Mark yelling into the phone on the other end, but I just could not control it. I was not there. No one could get in touch with me. My biggest fear and worst nightmare since I was first pregnant with Daniel was that I would not be able to get to my children immediately when they needed me. I had horrible night terrors, awakening, screaming that I could not get to them when the kids were little. Just when I thought that fear had passed, I was living it.

I tried to catch my breath and gather my thoughts. I was just over two hours away from them and had too many glasses of wine. While I was not drunk by any stretch, it was not appropriate for me to be driving anywhere. This was sobering me up pretty quickly though. As I grabbed the phone again, I started gathering my things to head back to Connecticut for a few days. I had no idea what to expect, so I started to throw an entire suitcase together. I also put on a cup of coffee since I was going to need the caffeine driving this late.

I told Mark that I was heading that way as soon as I could get my things together and in the car. He tried to talk me out of coming so late, but there was nothing that was going to stop me from being there tonight. I had already failed not being there when they called and needed me. I could not make that same mistake again. I found out which hospital they were at and told him I would be there in a couple of hours or less.

As I hung up the phone, I realized that I had never asked about him or Michele or their injuries. It was probably for the best as I was already overthinking and playing Jordyn's injuries in my head and envisioning what she looked like. It was probably better that I was not doing the same with all three of them.

It's amazing that even with no traffic and the ability to go too fast, the ride felt like an eternity. I tried driving with loud music and the window open, singing to every song, but I could not drown out the thoughts that were flooding my brain. What if? What if that driver had been going just a little faster? What if the car was not built as well as it was? What if no one had called 911 and they had been trapped there for a long time or the car had caught on fire? What if?

Mark always said that I was a worrier, that I had always worried about the "what-ifs." I told him that I was a realist. That these things happened and I wanted to try to prevent them from happening to our family. Of course, I was not there to do that this time. I had left. I left my family alone, and one of those "what-ifs" happened. I didn't blame Mark. I didn't blame the drunk driver. I blamed myself. I left!

If I had been there, we would have never been going out to a movie. We would have been doing what we always did on a Saturday night. It was always '80s movie night with junk food and popcorn. We all got into our PJ's, threw all the pillows and blankets on the floor, and sat around the coffee table watching the classic '80s movies. The kids knew all the words to *Breakfast Club* and *Pretty in Pink* at this point. One time, Daniel suggested that we move into the twenty-first century and watch something newer. There was a resounding "No Way" from the rest of the family. No one ever made that suggestion again!

I laughed at the memories of all of us in our pajamas week after week, year after year. It had become a tradition with us. When the kids got to be older and all their friends started going out on the weekends, they were torn between wanting to go out with their friends and being with the cool kids and being home for our traditional movie night. I loved that they wanted to continue and were so conflicted, but I also did not want them to have to make those decisions, so we cut it down to every other week for a while. After some time, we had cut back to occasionally then went back to weekly as they started to finish high school and move on.

I was wishing with everything that I had that I could close my eyes and wake up in front of the TV surrounded by my family and that this was all just a bad dream. A bad dream of my doing that just seemed to continue to worsen. Just as I was starting to feel a little better about my decision, I was slapped back to reality with a brick to the head.

When I got to the hospital, I parked and all but ran into the emergency room. I saw Daniel sitting in the waiting room with Michele lying on his lap. Both were sleeping. I immediately started to cry. I walked over and touched Daniel on the arm and smoothed Michele's hair off her face, trying carefully not to touch the cuts that were covered in what appeared to be antibiotic cream.

Daniel woke up and said, "Hey, Mom. Are you okay?"

I smiled. It was so like him to worry about me, knowing that I was probably an internal wreck. He was not wrong. "I'm better now!" I smiled back at him, trying not to allow my inner self to be heard screaming in agony.

Michele woke up and looked around as if she could not figure out where she was. As she started to remember, she looked up and saw me and jumped up, wrapping her arms around my neck. "Mom, it was terrible! I have never been so scared!" She was sobbing and would not let go of me. I wanted to squeeze her back, but not knowing the extent of her injuries, I did not want to hurt her.

"Honey," I said as I pulled back and looked her over. "I just want to see that you are okay. Are you hurt? Other than the few cuts on your face, is anything broken?" That was when I realized that her leg was bandaged.

"I ended up with a few stitches on my leg," she said, looking away from me.

"A few?" Daniel blurted out. "More like sixty!"

"*What*?" I said through my teeth as I exhaled, trying not to be sick. "Let me see!" I tried looking at her leg, but it was bandaged from her mid-thigh down to her mid-calf. "What hit you? Dad said you were in the back seat!"

Just as I asked, Mark walked into the waiting room. "Hey, I am so happy to see you! Jordyn just came back, and there is definitely a fracture in her pelvis. They said it should heal just fine on its own. She should just need some physical therapy."

"Oh, thank God!" I said. But then I saw the look on his face. "But...what are you not saying, Mark?"

"She is going to need surgery for her arm, and it looks like she may have ruptured her spleen. She has had some severe pain in her side, and there are indications from quick ultrasounds that she has some bleeding or seepage into her abdomen. They, at minimum, want to do exploratory surgery to ensure that it is not a slow bleed, given that her blood work is coming back irregular."

"I want to see her," I said as I stood up. Michele was still clinging onto me, so I hugged her and told her that I would be right back. I just needed to see Jordyn before they took her into surgery so she knew that I was here.

I walked back with Mark to Jordyn's room. As we walked, I looked him over. "Are you okay?" I asked. I could see that he had some cuts and a bruise on his arm, but I did not see any stitches.

He looked very tired, and I have never seen him looking as old as he did tonight. It suddenly dawned on me that I was so wrapped up in my own thoughts, but it was Mark that was driving when all this happened.

I stopped and grabbed his hand. "It was not your fault!" I said.

He looked at me and said, "I have never been so scared as right after the accident. The last thing I heard before the crash was Jordyn screaming. Then it was just the sound of metal screaming and glass breaking. We were being thrown around the car, and then it just stopped. All of it just stopped. There was no noise, no movement. I was so scared to open my eyes and find them dead. I just…" He started crying, and I grabbed him and held him. "I'm so sorry, I'm so sorry. I never saw her—"

"Mark, there was nothing that you could have done. You said that she came out of nowhere. You know that coming over the hill, you don't see the stop until the last minute. If she was going too fast, you would not see her until the last minute. You cannot blame yourself! The girls are going to be just fine. What about you? Do you have any injuries?"

He stepped back, still shaking, and shook his head. "No, I don't think so. I was bounced around a bit, and the few minutes after we stopped are a bit blurry, but I don't think I hit anything. Everything hurts but is numb right now. I don't even know if that makes sense." He looked so small and confused, much like Daniel looked when he was small and there was something overwhelming happening.

"Well, you were just in a car accident, and your emotions are running high. Not to mention that it is almost morning, so you have also been up for nearly twenty-four hours. It is to be expected that you are sore and numb. Why don't you go take a nap in the waiting room with the kids? I just want to see Jordyn before they take her to surgery. I need to see her for myself and make sure that she knows that I am here."

"Of course! I will just wait for you out there. Give her a kiss for me and tell her that we are all waiting for her." He turned to head back down the hall. "Oh, and, Laura," he had turned around to look at me, "thank you for coming back. We really needed you!" He smiled at me and walked away.

I knew that he was sincere and not at all trying to be hurtful, but that comment cut like a machete. I should not have had to come back. I should have been here. My family needed me, and I was not there for them.

Walking into her room, I was trying to prepare myself for the worst. But seeing Jordyn in that big bed, with all the monitors on her, she looked so small. I don't think any mother is ever prepared to see their child like this. She was bruised on the entire right side of her body. Her right arm was wrapped in a bandage and a sling across her chest. She was wincing in her sleep, obviously in pain. I sat down next to her bed, not wanting to disturb any sleep she was able to get. I looked at the board on the wall, noting that she was a fall risk and the schedule for her surgery, as well as pre-op plans. I could see that she was on an IV and hoped that they had given her medication to ease the pain. I sat in the chair next to her and slid it as close to her bed as I could without disturbing any monitors. I touched her left hand gently, trying not to hurt her. She flinched a little then settled when I just placed my hand over hers. I stared at her for what felt like hours.

The nurse came into the room and smiled at me. "You must be Mom," she said.

"I am! How is she? Did she get anything for the pain?" I did not want to bombard her with questions, but I needed to know everything.

"She has been given an antibiotic as well as pain medication. We also gave her a little something to help her sleep. She is scheduled to have surgery as soon as the surgeon arrives. The OR is being prepped right now. I just need to take her vitals. The surgeon and the anesthesiologist are going to want to speak to you or your husband before they take her in."

"Of course!" I said. "Anything that you need, just let me know." I felt rude, but I could not take my eyes off Jordyn. I was afraid that if I did, something might happen to her.

Jordyn started to stir a little, and when she moved, she cried out in pain. I jumped up and looked at the nurse. "I thought she had pain meds!" I said. Instantly, I heard the accusatory tone of my voice. "I'm sorry, I did not mean for that to come out sounding so mean!"

"You are fine. I completely understand. My daughter was in an accident, and I was a wreck! Even being a nurse, it was hard not being able to fix her. I was terrible to her nurses!" She reassured me. "We did give her pain meds, but it has been a few hours, and she is just about due for another dose. I will go get it now."

As she left the room, Jordyn opened one eye, looking around aimlessly. I was not sure if she was awake or coherent, but I wanted to make sure she knew I was there. I stood up and moved into her line of vision.

"Hi, baby," I whispered to her. "Mom is here. How are you feeling?"

Jordyn moved a little, but every time that she did, she cried out. I told her. "Try not to move. The nurse is getting some more pain medicine. You are going to be sore for a while." I was smiling, trying to reassure her that everything was going to be fine. It was the total opposite of how I was actually feeling, but I was putting on a good show.

"Mom?" Jordyn groaned.

"Yes, baby, I am right here." I took her hand again. "I'm not going anywhere."

Jordyn settled back down just as the nurse came back with her medication. "She was just awake but is really in a lot of pain." I told the nurse.

"I would expect that with her injuries. She was very lucky!" the nurse said as she injected the pain medication into Jordyn's IV.

I could see Jordyn's body relaxing as the medication started to take effect. *They were all very lucky*, I thought. I don't even want to think about how much worse this could have been for all of them. If that person had been going any faster, I may not be sitting here right now. Tears came to my eyes again, and this time, I just let them flow. I had seen everyone, and they were all going to be just fine. Now I just needed to figure out if we, collectively, were going to be alright.

I met with the surgeon and the anesthesiologist, and before they took her off to surgery, I kissed Jordyn and told her that we were all waiting for her and that we loved her. I walked out of the room and down the hall, but I did not go all the way to the waiting room. I really just needed a moment alone to process it all.

I was not a religious person, but I had certainly found myself talking to the universe and asked for a lot of help today! I found myself walking down the hall to the hospital chapel. I sat in the back and stared at the altar and stained-glass window. I heard a noise behind me and turned to see Daniel standing in the doorway.

Daniel was the quiet one. He was very outgoing and sociable, but he was observant. He could work a room at a party and still be able to tell who was arguing quietly, who was not having a good time, and could tell when two people were really into one another. I knew just from his presence in the doorway that he was picking up on my feelings. Not the obvious feelings of fear and anxiety over the accident and my family's injuries but my guilt over it all.

"You know it is not your fault Mom, right?" he said as he sat down next to me in the back of the chapel. He placed his arm around my shoulder, and I leaned back into him.

"How did you get so smart?" I asked him, trying to sound funny. "I know, honey, but I should have been there."

"Mom, it would have happened whether you were there or not! Or even worse, you could have been in that car. Then what would everyone do without you to take care of everyone?"

"Did you talk to your sisters? Are they upset with me?" I asked but afraid to know the answer.

"Mom, you are the only one upset with you! They were just happy to see you. We all were! I don't ever want to get that kind of call again! I cannot even imagine how you felt being so far away. I know that is your biggest fear." He looked at me with a sad, concerned face.

"It most definitely is. I guess looking at it as glass half full, now I know how I handled being put in that situation. I would prefer not to do it again! It was terrifying." We both sat back just staring ahead at the stained glass, both lost in our own thoughts.

When we finally walked back to the waiting room, Mark and Michele were both sleeping peacefully. A nurse must have brought down blankets for them both as they were sleeping in their respective chairs. I was trying hard not to think about the number of germs that was likely on those chairs and was just grateful that they were able to get some rest after what they had been through.

Daniel must have been reading my mind because he looked at me and said, "You should try to close your eyes for a while too, Mom. You've had a long night, and I'm sure tomorrow is going to be another rough one."

I turned and smiled at him and said, "I'm not even sure I could sleep at this point. Not until your sister is out of surgery." I glanced at my watch and said, "Oh, hey, Dunkin' should be open for coffee now! I wonder if we could get someone to deliver it to us here. It's a hospital, I'm sure they deliver all the time!"

Daniel looked out the window and back at me and said, "Mom, it is literally across the street. We could probably open the window and yell our order."

"I know, but I am afraid to leave this area until I have heard from the doctor about Jordyn's surgery results." I was pacing the room. I had never been able to go too far from a situation for fear of something happening and I would miss it. It was the same fear of not being able to get to my family. I knew it was probably a control kind of thing, but it was terrifying to me.

Daniel asked, "What do you want? I will just run over and grab it. Do you want your usual coffee?"

"Yes, please. But, Daniel, *please* be careful running across the street. I could not handle something happening to you tonight too!"

He laughed. "Mom, seriously. I think I can handle walking across the street!" he called back as he was walking toward the exit. "Now what you should be worried about is my meeting up with a hot nurse and not making it back with your coffee!" He was laughing as he skipped down the hallway. He always had a way of making me feel better when things looked so dark. I was an optimist once. I was not sure what happened or when that changed.

I must have dozed a bit while I was lost in thought since the next thing I saw was the doctor walking into the waiting room. I sat up and wiped the drool from my lip. "Doctor, how is she?" I tried to keep my voice down, but it must have startled Mark awake. He sat up to listen too.

"She made it through surgery. We were able to find the bleed. He had a small tear in the artery going to her appendix. There was still enough blood flow that it does not seem to have damaged the appendix, but it was enough that it pooled in her abdomen. We were able to clean it up, stop the bleed, and while I was in the area, I checked to make sure there was no other damage. It all looked good although we did find a couple of fractured ribs. Those will heal on their own. They are really just painful. Otherwise, I expect she will make a full recovery. Obviously, we are going to hold her overnight since she is still in the recovery room. She will be there for another hour or so, and we will then take her upstairs to a room. I will want her to stay one more night, and if all goes well, she should be able to have the surgery on her arm on Monday. I want to wait until then to ensure that she does well after this surgery since it was exploratory and there was the bleed."

"Thank you, Doctor! When can we see her?" I asked, feeling very relieved but anxious because I wanted to see her.

"You can see her once she is back in her room. That will be another hour or so. But she will be sleepy and will likely sleep for the next several hours. You have all been through a lot tonight. You should go home and get some rest yourselves." He looked at Mark and said "Especially you two!" as he pointed to Michele. "Jordyn will have round-the-clock care. Go take care of yourselves now because she is going to need you!" He turned and walked away.

I turned and looked at Mark, already knowing he was looking at me. "Not a chance!" I said to him. "Not until I have seen her for myself. Maybe not at all." I was torn between wanting to go home with Mark and Michele because they had both been in the accident and had injuries of their own and staying with Jordyn who had the more serious injuries but was receiving professional care.

Daniel walked up with our coffees. "Oh, hey, you are awake. What did I miss?" he asked as he handed me my coffee. "I got you one too, Dad. I figured you would want it when you woke up."

"Thank you," said Mark. "Your sister is out of surgery. It went well. She had a bleed from a torn artery to her appendix, but she will be fine. She has to stay until they can do the arm surgery on Monday, so we are going to be needing a lot of this coffee!" He turned and sat back down in the spot where he had been sleeping. I could tell from looking at him that the day and night was starting to take its toll on him.

"Mark, why don't you let Daniel take you and Michele home to get some sleep? I have my car here. Jordyn is out of surgery, and as soon as I see her for myself and know that she is doing well, I will head back to the house myself." I looked at Mark, pleading with my eyes, and glanced at Michele. I wanted him to take her home so she could rest and start to heal from not only her injuries but the trauma of the night.

Mark took my hint and with a little reluctance; he nudged Michele awake and said, "Come on, kiddo, you really should get some real sleep."

She started to argue, saying she wanted to wait until Jordyn was out of surgery, but Mark filled her in on the update and said that there was nothing that any of us could do at the moment. He looked to me for reassurance.

"Dad's right, honey. I will stay and see Jordyn once she is in her room, and I will make sure she is all set and knows that we were all here. Then I will come back to the house to make sure everyone is settling in and eating. We can all come back to the hospital later in the day after Jordyn has had some rest as well as the rest of us." I kissed her on the forehead and reassured her that I would be along shortly.

Daniel put his arm around her shoulder and walked her toward the exit. Mark stopped in front of me with a look of pure exhaustion and defeat.

"We will all be fine. I promise!" I said to him as I hugged him gently, still uncertain of how much he had been hurt during the crash. He stepped away, looked at me, and headed down the hall in the direction of the exit.

I was alone with my thoughts again. I was trying to concentrate on my coffee. It is amazing how good coffee tastes when you are tired, mind and body. Daniel was right, there was nothing that I could have done even if I had been here. I just had to make sure that I was here to take care of things now. Everyone was going to need help to recover from this, especially Jordyn. Things were still uncertain on her recovery, and she still had another surgery to go through. I will need to speak with her team of doctors to figure out what the recovery process was going to look like for both surgeries. That would also mean that we would need to deal with her school. I was not sure if they would hold her room if she was away for too long or if we had to withdraw her from this semester. So many things to figure out.

As I was reeling in my head about all the things to do, the nurse came out into the waiting room, looking around as if confused. "Are you Jordyn's mother?"

"I am," I said. "Her father and the other two went home to get some sleep. I wanted to make sure that I could see her before I headed there as well. Can I see her now?"

"Yes. We have moved her upstairs to her own room. She is on the fourth floor in W426. The visiting hours have not started, but under the circumstances, you can go and stay with her in her room. The nurse can also put a cot in there for you if you would like, or there is a chair that lays down and is rather comfortable. Just ask at the nurses' station if you need anything at all."

"Thank you so much," I said.

"I wish you and your family the best of luck and Jordyn a speedy recovery. She did very well. She is definitely a strong young lady!"

"I don't know where she gets that from!" I laughed. "Thank you again."

The nurse headed back to the recovery area, and I headed to the elevators to try to find Jordyn's room. I know that I had promised Michele that I would go back to the house as soon as I had seen Jordyn and knew that she was alright, but the sound of a nap next to her for a little while just to catch my brain up was sounding very good right now. I would have to decide once I got up to the room and saw how she was doing.

I found the floor and her ward pretty easily. I was wandering looking for the room when a nurse was coming down the hallway with a monitor and a handful of medicines. "Are you by chance Jordyn's mother?" she asked me.

"I am!" I said, feeling quite relieved that I could get help to find her. The panic was setting in a bit with not being able to find her.

"Follow me, I was heading there myself." She led me back down the hallway that I had just gone down the wrong way. "It is easy to get lost with these room numbers. I'm pretty sure that the designer let their two-year-old pick the room numbers. They do not really make any sense!" She chuckled at her own joke. "Here we are. Go ahead and head in. I need to do some vitals and give her some more pain medication, but I will give you a minute alone with her. I will be back in a few." With that, she headed down the hall to the nurses' station.

I opened the door and peeked in, bracing myself against what I might find. As I stepped in, I heard a little voice, "Mom?"

"Oh, I was not expecting you to be awake! Hi, baby. How are you feeling?" I stepped to the side of her bed. She looked tired but better than I had expected given what she had been through in the last twelve hours.

"I'm okay," she squeaked. "I'm really thirsty, but they are saying that I cannot have anything to drink yet." She stopped and licked her lips. You could tell from her lips and the way that she was speaking that her mouth was extremely dry. "Where is Dad? Is Michele okay? I don't remember much."

I reached over and touched her non-broken hand. "They are both fine. Daniel took them home to get some sleep. Dad just had a few bumps and bruises, and Michele needed some stitches. They are both going to be fine. How are you feeling right now? You have been through quite a bit!"

"I'm so sore, and I feel like I weigh an extra 100 lbs." She lifted her arm that was wrapped in a sling. "This is fun. What is wrong with it?"

"You broke it in a few places, and they are going to need to do surgery. But they have to wait for you to recover enough from this past surgery." She looked at me with a blank stare as if she was not understanding what I was saying to her. "Honey, you do know that you just got out of surgery, right?"

She looked at me for another minute or so and slowly said, "I think I remember something. Everything is so foggy and feels like it was all just a dream. I remember being in the car and seeing headlights. Then the next real clear thing I remember is seeing you walking in. I have flashes of broken glass, then sirens, and Dad yelling. I remember flashes of firemen and the ambulance. Then I know I was in the emergency room, but then it goes really black." She looked away as if she was trying to put the pieces together and remember something solid.

"Honey, when they did the scans on you and found your broken arm, they checked the rest of you since you took the brunt of the impact. They found a spot that looked concerning, so they did exploratory surgery. They found that there was damage to an artery that went to your appendix that was causing some blood to leak into your abdomen. They stopped the bleeding. While they were in there, they discovered a couple of broken ribs also."

"Well, that would explain why I feel like my stomach is all blown up and it's kind of numb!" She tried to move a bit in the bed but let out a gasp at the pain.

"Don't try to move yet. Between the crash and being tossed around the car and the surgery, everything is going to hurt! The nurse was going to be coming back in shortly to check your vitals and give you some more pain medication anyway." She stopped and drifted off again. "Jordyn, don't try to force your memory. It will come back on its own. We are all here, and you are safe. You have been through a lot in the last twelve hours. Just try to get some sleep to let your body heal, and you can think about it more tomorrow."

"Are you going to stay with me?" she asked. She had the look on her face that she would always get when she was young. She was fiercely independent when she had me behind her to make sure that she would be alright.

"I will stay as long as you need me!" I smiled and kissed her on the forehead. "The nurse said that the chair right there lays out, and it is actually pretty comfy."

Just as I said it, her nurse came in with the medication. "She was not wrong! I have had to sleep in one a time or two! How are you feeling, Jordyn? What is your pain level on a scale of 1 to 10?"

"It is probably a 5 if I don't move. When I move, it is a 12! But I am terribly thirsty. Is there anything that I can drink?" she asked.

"You are not to have any food or liquids for twenty-four hours after your abdominal surgery, just to ensure that there were no other issues and they did not need to go back in. I can let you have ice chips. Just make sure that you do not drink the melted ice. Just let them melt in your mouth slowly."

Jordyn eagerly jumped at the chance to have anything. "I can do that! Thank you."

The nurse gave Jordyn her pain medication and took her vitals. She then went back out and came back with a pillow and blanket for me and some ice chips for Jordyn. As she was leaving, she let us know that the next shift was going to be coming on soon, so she would not see Jordyn until later tonight.

It was then that I realized how late it had become. I was so wrapped up with Jordyn and finally being able to talk to her that I had not realized it was nearly 7:00 a.m. I fed Jordyn some ice chips and watched as she started to doze off. I closed all the blinds tight to block the light and dimmed her lights, leaving just the night-light on, knowing that the nurses would be in almost hourly to check vitals. I then settled into my makeshift bed in the chair. I wanted to make sure that Mark knew that Jordyn was doing fine and that I was staying with her for a bit.

I did not want to wake him in case he was finally sleeping, so I sent him a text. "Hey, Jordyn is doing well. She was awake when I got in to see her. She is sore and a bit foggy on all of the details but otherwise good. She asked me to stay with her, so I'm going to camp out for a bit. She is on the fourth-floor room W426. I will text you when we wake up."

I put my phone next to me, laid my hand on Jordyn's, and fell asleep.

Sleep was short-lived as the nurses were in continuously to take Jordyn's vitals. I was in and out of sleep, aware that they were in the room and that they were not concerned with anything that they were seeing. I was relieved knowing that she was under constant care, so I was able to maintain a drowsy partial state of sleep. I must have fallen into a deep sleep at some point because I was awakened by Mark and Michele talking to Jordyn.

As I sat up, Mark turned and said, "Hey, welcome to the party!"

I sat up looking around. I noticed that the sun was fairly high in the sky and there was a lot of activity in the hallway.

"What time is it?" I asked no one in particular.

"It's almost ten. You must have been tired! You didn't even stir when we came in," Michele said. "I can't believe that you slept at all. We were taking bets on the way over as to whether you would be sleeping or sitting guard over Jordyn when we got here. I lost!" Michele laughed.

"I am not sure what happened," I said. "The last I knew there were nurses in and out, and I was listening to each of their assessments. I'm not sure when I actually fell asleep." I sat up, trying to straighten myself up and not feel like I needed another ten hours of sleep.

"The doctor was in the hallway when we were coming in," Mark said. "He is very pleased with how her vitals have been, so it looks like she should be able to have the surgery tomorrow. But they want to do an ultrasound today to make sure that there are no signs of bleeding in her abdomen still."

I looked at Jordyn. "How are you feeling? Did you get any sleep last night? Between the nurses poking and prodding that is."

Jordyn looked at me. "I dozed here and there. I asked if there was something that they could give me to help me sleep, but because of the anesthesia, they said that they could not for twenty-four hours. Thankfully, the pain meds do help in that department a little, so I slept on and off. I cannot wait to be home in my bed so I can sleep for two days straight!" She laughed.

"Well, once you have had your other surgery and they release you, we will get you home, set up, and you can sleep as long as you would like! It will be good for your healing too!" I smiled at her. Getting her home was my biggest priority right now. I just had not thought about the repercussions of that. It was her home still, but it was not mine anymore.

I needed to be there to take care of her once she was home, but how was I going to do that? I could not just say, "Hey, Mark, I'm going to move back for a few weeks to take care of Jordyn, then I will be out of your hair again!" We had not spoken in a bit, so that conversation was not going to be that easy.

I looked up to Mark looking at me. It was as if he could tell what I was thinking. He had a soft look in his eyes, and he smiled a little smile at me as if to say, "Don't worry about it, we will figure it out as we go." I smiled back but happy was not at all how I was feeling. I had thought we were past all this uneasy feeling and that things would be easier for me to come back as I needed to. But the more that I was away and the less that Mark and I communicated, especially after an argument, it just made things more uncomfortable when we were thrown back together.

I excused myself to go try to freshen up and not feel like I had slept on a park bench somewhere. Then I headed down the hallway to find some coffee. Hospital coffee was not at all on my list of desires, but I was not ready to face sunlight and walk across the street yet. I heard footsteps coming down the hallway behind me, and I already knew who they belonged to without needing to turn around.

"Hey, wait up," Mark said. "I could use another cup of coffee myself."

I slowed to let Mark catch up although in all honesty, I was trying to escape seeing him at this point as much as I needed coffee. "Sorry, I should have asked if anyone else wanted one. I guess I'm still half asleep." I joked.

"No worries. I just wanted to grab you for a minute without anyone else around." That was what I was trying to avoid, and he was trying to cause it to happen. "How are you doing with all of this? I know that I threw it at you really quickly and you did not have any real time to process it before driving all this way to come see us. Are you alright?"

I stopped and looked at him. This was typical of Mark. He was one that always worried about everyone else. He was the one in the accident. He saw the girls after when they were trapped in the car, the broken glass, the blood, the ambulance, and fire trucks. Yet here he was worried how I was handling all of it.

"I am okay. I'm still very tired and probably will be for weeks, but I'm fine! You are all okay, and after another surgery, Jordyn will heal just fine. I just wish I had been here…" My voice trailed off, and I could feel the tears coming again.

Mark stepped forward and wrapped his arms around my shoulders. "Laura, don't. Do not do that to yourself. There is nothing that you could have done even if you had been here! I was the one driving. I didn't see her. Plus, if you had been there, that could have been you in the front seat, and God knows how things could have been different. Jordyn saw her coming and reacted. The paramedic said that probably saved her life from the amount of damage to her door."

I tried not to listen to those details because the thought of it being worse terrified me. I clung to Mark and let myself cry. It was apparently what I was needing because it felt like it soothed my soul. You know that kind of cry where you just let out everything that has been building for as long as you can remember? That cry that encompasses all of what you thought you had worked through and had moved on from, but then one thing happens that causes you to cry and you let out every emotion that you were holding onto and even some that you did not realize that you had. This was that.

When I was finally able to regain my composure, I pulled back away from Mark and dried my face. "I am so sorry! I don't know where that came from!" I lied. I actually knew exactly where it came from, and that was the deepest part of my being, from my exhausted inner self that had been fighting for months to breathe. It had come from months of buildup of watching my life just crumble around me, of my own doing, and just standing there watching it fall without moving.

"Do not apologize! Laura, I have always been here for you. I still am. I have never left, and I am not planning on going anywhere. So any time that you feel the need to let go, I am here."

"Well, thank you. Apparently, I really needed that. It seems long overdue," I said as I straightened myself back up and tried to look him in the eye again. I was not sure why I was not able to look at him. I knew that I was embarrassed by what had just happened, but that had never stopped me before. Maybe I just did not want him to see me vulnerable again, but why? Was I afraid that if I allowed him to see vulnerability, in any situation, that I would let him back in? I was honestly not sure that he was ever out!

This was not the place that I wanted to have any of these thoughts or discussions. I needed to focus on Jordyn and her recovery. That had to be my only concern right now. I did not have the time or the energy to expend on anything else.

"I really need to get some coffee so that I can feel somewhat human again!" I said as I started to walk again. I was stopped by Mark grabbing my arm and pulling me back to him.

"Please don't shut me out again, Laura! This family has been through enough in the last twenty-four hours. We need each other more than ever. *They*," he said pointing back toward Jordyn's room, "They need both parents now. We need to work together as a team again to make sure that we fix everything for them. I need you to be part of this team again. I cannot do it without you, Laura. Please don't make me." Mark let his arms fall to his side, and he hung his head down. It was his turn to cry.

I stepped forward and hugged him as he had done for me. He had been through so much more than I had last night and over the past few months. I at least owed it to him to let him have his moment of weakness and soul-cleansing cry, and I would comfort him.

As I hugged him, I realized that I had caused this for him. I was upset because my world was ripped apart, but so was his. As many times as I had thought about it before, it had not become as real as it was right in this moment, standing just feet from our daughter's hospital room. So many things had happened since I made the decision to leave. It felt as if the universe was telling me something. Maybe it was time for me to listen.

Once Mark had regained his composure, we simply looked at each other and smiled. We did not need to even talk about it. We turned and started walking toward the cafeteria when I changed direction.

"Let's go get real coffee," I said, heading for the doors to go across the street. After everything that had just happened in the hall, I needed to get out and feel the sun.

When we got back to the room, we found Michele lying in bed with Jordyn watching cartoons, just like they did when they were little. Mark and I laughed as we started recalling stories of when the kids were little. It was as if reliving those memories of our family and a happier time would help to heal some of the pain that we have been through recently.

Later in the day, after an ultrasound that showed no signs of continued bleeding, it was decided that Jordyn would have the additional surgery on her arm the next day. Everyone was getting bored and hungry, and Jordyn was getting sleepy. Since she was still not able to eat anything, we decided that it would not be fair to her to order and eat in front of her. So we agreed to go out to grab dinner and let her get some sleep. I still wanted to stay with her for the night so that I could be there when she left for surgery in the morning, so I drove separately and met everyone at the restaurant. I was a bit uneasy leaving Jordyn's side, but I also knew that she would not sleep with us in the room.

We went to our favorite restaurant that was a staple for our family. It was our go-to place when we did not want to cook. The staff and owners had become like family. I had not given it much thought when we decided to go here since it was safe and familiar, but now standing out front, I was hesitant to go in knowing that things were different. I did not know if Mark and the kids had been here since I left or how much anyone at the restaurant knew about our current situation.

I walked in the door. Mark and Michele had beat me there and were in our usual spot. Daniel was walking up to the table from the counter. *Just smile and walk,* I told myself as I hoped that no one noticed me. I made it to the table before Peter and Danielle, the owners, noticed me.

"LAURA!" They both shrieked in unison.

Danielle ran over to hug me. Well, I guess that they did know about our situation. I hugged Danielle and smiled at Peter standing by the table.

"It's so good to see you guys!" I smiled, hoping that they were not going to start asking questions that I was not able to answer at this time.

Thankfully, Peter launched into talking to Mark, and Danielle joined in, so there were no questions thrown my way. Danielle headed back to the kitchen when one of the waitresses called for her. One of the waitresses that was new enough that I did not know came over to the table to take our drink order. I was thankful that I would not have anyone else that may question about the last few months.

After Peter was called back to the kitchen, Mark turned to me and whispered under his breath "You're welcome" and smiled at me. I gave him a questioning look. He said that just before I had arrived, Peter asked where you were. He told him that I was right behind them and left it at that.

The rest of dinner was uneventful and fairly quiet for this group. Everyone seemed to be lost in their own thoughts. It was possible that everyone was just tired as well. It had still been a long twenty-four hours, and it was going to be a long road ahead of us. Jordyn was going to take some time to heal as were Mark and Michele. Their wounds would probably heal quickly, but mentally, it was going to take some time. It had probably not really hit either of them completely yet since we were still dealing with Jordyn being in the hospital and her upcoming surgery.

We said our goodbyes to Danielle and Peter and headed outside. I said good night to Daniel before he left, and I was on my way to say good night to Michele when she started to cry. I put my arms around her and told her that we were all here and her sister was going to be fine.

"That is not why I'm upset!" she cried.

"Then what is wrong?" I asked.

"I miss this…us. All of us! I want you to come home!"

I continued to hug her and just looked at Mark. He was trying not to look at me, but I could see his face.

I didn't know what to say, so I said the first thing that came to mind. "Well, I am here right now, and it looks like I will be for a little while, at least as long as Jordyn and you need me to be here."

"So like forever!" Michele said very matter-of-factly.

I smiled as I continued to hug her, too tired to argue the point right now. Mark looked over at me as if to see what I would say. I just looked back at him with the look of "What can I say?"

As I headed back to the hospital and the rest of the family headed home, I had to wonder exactly what the plan was going to be. I had honestly not thought far beyond Jordyn's surgeries and knowing that she was going to be okay. I had not considered what would happen once she was released from the hospital other than the fact that I knew that I was going to take care of her. No one can take care of a sick or injured child like their mother, and I was not going to let anyone else do it. I had just not considered that I would need to move back to the house to do so. I had not discussed it with Mark, and I had not thought about the logistics. Then how long is long enough? Do I just plan a week? Two weeks? I cannot really set a limit, but how long is long enough?

I had not put enough thought into any of this. I honestly just jumped in knowing that I had to do something, and here I was. I would need to talk to Mark once Jordyn's surgery was over and we had an idea of how long she would be staying in the hospital. I would also need to call work tomorrow and explain why I was not going to be in and how long I was going to be out. So I really needed to try to figure things out all the way around.

I got back to the hospital still feeling out of sorts. I was always the planner. I knew what I was doing every step of the way. In the last few months, I was really off my game. Winging it was not in my vocabulary or my comfort zone.

I walked into Jordyn's room to find her still awake and watching TV. "Hey, there, did you get any sleep while I was gone?" I asked her.

She smiled. "Yes, I actually just woke up a little while ago. How was dinner? I need you to describe it in great detail because I am *starving*!"

I laughed and kissed her forehead. "I will not torture you like that. We went to Nina's, so the usual. It was nice to see Danielle and Peter," I said as I prepared my bed for the night.

"Oh? How was that? It has to be a little awkward…given the circumstances." I winced at those words. Thankfully, I was turned away from Jordyn so that she could not see my expression.

"It was fine," I said. I was not entirely lying. They had not asked any uncomfortable questions, only hinted to the fact that I had not been around lately.

"Well, that's good. Mom, I'm sorry that you keep getting pulled back here. I know that you left for a reason. I still am not entirely certain that I know what that reason is, but I respect your decisions. I just miss you, and I really appreciate that you came back for me. I am so happy to have you here through this!" Jordyn looked at me with tears in her eyes.

"Baby, I would not be anywhere else! I will always be here for you, no matter what! Time and distance will *never* keep me from being here anytime that you need me." I looked at her, wondering when she had turned into this woman that was sitting in front of me. Last night, looking at her in the hospital bed, she looked so small and helpless. Now she was sounding like such a mature adult. I smiled and walked into the bathroom to get ready for bed.

When I came out, Jordyn had dozed off. I kissed her forehead and turned out the lights. I decided to leave the TV on for the background noise and a distraction from my thoughts. I knew that I had decisions to make, but tonight they could wait. My brain needed a break. Tomorrow morning, Jordyn will go to surgery. Once she was out and we had word about how it went and what her recovery was going to look like from both surgeries, I would be able to make some decisions.

I lay in bed, watching crappy TV because the remote control was attached to Jordyn's bed and I did not want to disturb her. I must have drifted off pretty quickly because I did not remember more than one commercial before I was being awoken by the nurse coming in to start preparing Jordyn for surgery. I sat up, rubbing my eyes, and asked what time it was.

"It is six thirty," the nurse said. "We are starting to take her vitals and get her prepared to head to surgery. The doctor has the OR scheduled for eight." She turned to Jordyn and said, "The anesthesiologist will be in to talk to you and have you sign a consent even though they just did a surgery yesterday morning. Once that is all set, the doctor should be in to discuss the surgery. Then we can get you down to the operating room."

"Sounds good," Jordyn said, looking at her arm. "I will be glad to have this fixed so it can start healing and this can all be behind me!"

The nurse turned to me and said, "You can wait right here. We will bring her back here after surgery and once they release her from the recovery room. I will come in and give you updates, and then when the doctor does his rounds later, you can ask any questions that you have for him at that time." She smiled and headed out the door.

"Well, good morning!" I smiled and looked at Jordyn. "I guess this will be over pretty soon! I can imagine you will be happy to be able to eat again!"

"You have no idea! I had not eaten before we left to go to the movies because we were grabbing food there. So breakfast Saturday was the last time that I ate! I could eat an entire menu at this point!"

"I will be happy to get you whatever you want once this is over. But I am thinking that they are probably going to start you off slowly with probably a liquid diet just because of what your poor abdomen has been through in the last couple of days. So just be prepared."

Jordyn groaned at this.

"Sorry, kiddo, but I did not want to give you any false hopes of having a big fat sub for dinner tonight."

Jordyn flung her head back against the bed. "Well, then, I hope that they give me something to knock me out for a really long time because I want to be able to wake up and eat!"

"I can partially oblige that request," laughed a tall man in a lab coat walking in the door. He stretched out his hand and introduced himself to me. "Hi, I'm Dr. Damon, and I will be Jordyn's anesthesiologist today." He reached his hand out to Jordyn, too, then turned back to me. "You must be Jordyn's sister."

I laughed out loud. "Oh no, I am Mom!"

"Well, you definitely do not look old enough to be her mother!" Dr. Handsome said.

I was not sure if he was just being funny and trying to make the situation easier or if he was actually flirting.

He turned to Jordyn and talked to her about the procedure and what to expect as well as the after care and recovery. He then turned to me and asked if I had any questions.

"No, I don't think so. Jordyn, do you have any questions?" I said, trying to take his attention off of me again. While it was cute and endearing, it was becoming awkward in front of my daughter.

"No, I think I'm good. I just hope that you are more focused in the operating room," Jordyn said to him and then feigned a laugh.

I could feel myself turning beet red and just stared at Jordyn with my best mom face. She stared back and shrugged her shoulders as if to say "What?"

The doctor left the room, and I could not help but to blurt out, "What was that? Like could you be any more obvious? And you, what were you thinking calling him out like that?"

"Calling who out on what?" came from behind me. I turned around to see Mark standing in the door. "Good morning, sweetheart," he said to Jordyn. "I was hoping to catch you before you headed into surgery."

"You just missed the anesthesiologist, but I have not seen the doctor yet. He should be coming in any time," Jordyn said back as she smiled across at me.

"So what were you guys talking about when I walked in? Something about calling someone out on something," Mark asked.

I shot Jordyn a look as if to tell her not to say anything.

"Oh, nothing," Jordyn said. I felt instant relief. Then she said, "Just the anesthesiologist hitting on Mom!" Jordyn laughed, thinking it was funny. That also could have been the medication that they put in her IV to relax her a little before the surgery.

Mark shot me a look that I tried to pretend that I had not noticed. In the meantime, I shot Jordyn a look. Then I turned toward Mark. "I'm glad that you were able to get here before she headed into surgery. We also have not yet met with the doctor, so if you have any questions for him, now is the perfect time," I said, trying to change the subject.

Unfortunately, I knew Mark well enough to know that he would drop the subject for now, but as soon as we were alone, he would have a million questions.

Just as I finished saying it, the doctor walked in. "Well, look at this! It is the whole clan." He looked at Jordyn and said, "Are you ready, young lady?"

"I am more than ready! I just want to be done with this so I can eat!" Jordyn smiled at him, half joking and half serious.

The doctor went on to explain the surgery, the expected duration, and when she would be brought back to her room. "We are going to keep her overnight, just as a precaution because of the fact that she just had another surgery yesterday. We want to keep an eye on her and make sure that there are no issues. Also, because of the extent of the surgery, I will want to check her again in the morning before allowing her to go home. Then we will have her follow up in a week to take x-rays and make sure that the placement is still good for the hardware and that things are starting to heal properly. Do any of you have any questions?"

We all looked at each other and shook our heads no.

"Okay, good. Once surgery is over, I will call you on your cell, Laura, and give you an update on how the surgery went. Then the nurses will keep you updated after that. I am assuming that you will both be hanging around until she gets back?"

We both nodded our heads yes.

"Well, you are welcome to stay right here or go get coffee. I will call you either way. Jordyn," he said looking at her, "I will see you in a few minutes."

"Thank you, Doctor," we said at the same time and looked at each other and laughed. We both turned back to Jordyn to say our goodbyes and I love yous just as the nurses were coming in to take her to the operating room.

After she was gone, I turned to Mark and asked if he wanted to run now and grab a coffee. I knew I was going to need one not just because of the early hour but because he was going to start asking me a bunch of questions that were just ridiculous.

We walked down the hall and across the street, and while we were in line waiting to order our coffees, he turned and said, "So the doctor was hitting on you?"

There it was. I just looked at him like he was being ridiculous.

"Well, I guess you are moving up in the world!" Mark said and then turned as if he were done with the conversation.

"What is that supposed to mean?" I asked, now irritated by the entire discussion.

"Nothing, just that now you have doctors interested in you. It's an improvement over just an engineer like me!" Mark shrugged like it was no big deal. "I'm just saying. You could do worse!"

"First of all, Jordyn says he was flirting. I didn't see that at all. And second of all, it is not like he asked me to go out or we are dating or that we are getting married! You are being absolutely ridiculous. So what is your real problem, Mark?" I shot back at him a little more harshly than I had wanted it to be.

"Ouch, Laura. I don't know. What do you think my problem is? Maybe that my *wife* has not been home in months. That she just up and moved out one day with no warning or discussion. Or the fact that now other men are flirting with her and who knows what else, and I'm just supposed to laugh and act like I'm one of your girlfriends that you can tell these things to over a cup of coffee. Or that it is not supposed to hurt?" He was fighting back tears. "I don't know, Laura. What is my problem?"

"Wow!" was all that I was able to get out of my mouth. I just stood there staring at him. "I do not even know what to say to you right now. All of this from a stupid comment from our daughter who was high on pain medication as she was getting ready to head into her second major surgery in two days." I paused to continue to stare at this man that I was dumbfounded; he was being so self-centered at the moment. "And you thought *now* was a good time to have your breakdown? Now while we are waiting to hear how our daughter fares from surgery? Now while I am waiting and praying for my daughter's well-being? Are you sure that you really want to have this discussion right now?"

I stepped forward to order my coffee, and knowing that Mark was not able to communicate at the present moment, I ordered his as well. I also ordered a couple of breakfast sandwiches as I knew that we were going to need to eat something.

Mark stood next to me in silence while we waited for our order to be prepared. I could tell that he was torn between continuing the discussion that he had clearly been feeling the need to have with me and wanting to wait for a better time to have it.

I grabbed our food and coffees, handing him his items, and we started walking back in silence. Once we were back in Jordyn's room, I sat in my chair. Mark went over and sat on the spare chair. I took a sip of my coffee.

Mark turned to me and said, "I'm sorry. You are right. My timing was bad, but the doctor flirting with you just sent me off the deep end."

"Mark, do you have any idea how many men have flirted with me over the years? How many times did your coworker Brian flirt with me? At every company picnic, party, every time I stopped in your office. Hell, he was always trying to kiss me at the Christmas parties! There is nothing different with this one than any of those!" I said, trying to keep the irritation out of my voice.

"The difference is that now you can act on them!" Mark said, almost under his breath.

I stopped and looked at him. I was not sure what to say. The thought of John and our night out less than two days ago. I had not considered that a date, and I was not looking for any type of romance. I had taken vows that I still took very seriously. Until there were documents and an agreement between Mark and I, our vows remained intact. I wanted to say all that to Mark, minus the part about John obviously, but I did not want to open that can of worms about filing for divorce. I was not ready for that step yet. Although I still was not sure how that was any different than what we had right now.

Instead of continuing the discussion, I looked at him and said "Mark, it was just another guy and just another silly attempt to get something they knew they were not going to get." I then changed the subject asking how Michele was doing and whether she was going to be coming to the hospital at some point today.

After talking about Michele and a few other niceties trying just to keep the subject off what had just happened or the dozen other things that we needed to discuss, I decided that I needed to discuss the inevitable. "Mark, we need to talk about Jordyn coming home from here."

"I know. I would assume that you will want to be able to help take care of her when she gets home…at least for a little while," Mark said in a way that I could tell he was trying to get information.

"Yes, I would. But I also do not want you to be uncomfortable. After all, it is your home, and I am intruding," I said. As soon as it came out of my mouth, it sounded ridiculous.

Mark must have been able to read my face because he just looked at me with an odd look on his face and said, "What in the hell do you mean? Laura, that is *our* home! We created that home for our family, and it will always be ours! You are welcome to come home any time you want and stay as long as you want. I keep hoping that you will come home for good, but that is just my wishful thinking." His tone got quiet and somewhat reserved. "But really, please know that I would never say no to having you home. So you can stay as long as you need or want to. I would be happy to have you. You can still have the guest room. I have not touched it since the last time you stayed, except to wash the sheets."

It took me a minute to respond. I was lost in thought and trying to choke back my feelings. I had so much that I wanted to say, but I knew that I was tired and emotional right now, and I did not want to say something that I may have been feeling in the moment and regret it later. So I opted for "Thank you, Mark. I was dreading asking you because it really does seem like a lot to ask, given the circumstances with us. I appreciate you letting me be there to take care of her. It really means a lot!" I smiled at him. Mark smiled back at me and looked as if he was going to say something, but my phone rang interrupting him.

"Hello?" I said, motioning to Mark that it was work. I stepped out into the hallway to explain what had happened and that I was going to be out for a while. At the moment, I did not have a time-frame, but as soon as I knew what was happening and had a better idea of things, I would let them know.

When I finished, I went back into Jordyn's room. Mark was standing and staring out the window. "Do you believe that everything happens for a reason?" he asked. "I'm starting to think that it may be true." He turned back around to face me, but before he could continue his thought, my phone rang again. I looked at it but did not recognize the number.

"Hello?" I answered.

It was the doctor. I motioned to Mark that it was the doctor with the update and put the phone on speaker. The doctor advised that the surgery had gone well. There was a bit of a concern when her blood pressure dropped during surgery, but it could have just been the fact that she had undergone the other surgery in the last couple of days, so her body had not had an opportunity to recover from that anesthesia quite yet. Otherwise, she did very well. She was in recovery, and the nurse would advise shortly on how long until she would be brought back up to her room. He also advised that he would check on her later but that he would likely keep her for another two nights just to be safe and watch her with that blood pressure drop. He wanted to be safe. We thanked him for the update and hung up.

Both of us sat in silence for a few minutes, just absorbing the information that he had just given us. I was not sure how to react at the news that her pressure dropped during surgery. Now I had thoughts racing through my head, like was there another underlying issue? Was it really just that she had undergone the other surgery so recently? Could there be another bleed that they were not seeing? I was not a doomsday person, but I was cautious and consider worst-case scenarios so that I could be prepared. I would rather prepare for the worst and hope for the best.

Mark broke the silence first. "She is fine, Laura. She made it through surgery just fine and is in recovery. I know exactly what you are thinking." He looked at me. "We can talk to the doctor again about the possibility of an underlying condition, but just remember that the doctor is right. Her body has been through a lot in the last couple of days or less. It was probably just reacting to all of the stress."

"I know, you are probably right. But that concerns me. It obviously also concerned him because they are keeping her for an extra day." I was glad that they were just to be safe and so I could ask a lot more questions. Plus, it was one more day that I was not staying at the house with Mark. Not that I minded, but it was just awkward under the circumstances.

We turned on the TV waiting for Jordyn to return to her room although neither of us was actually watching it. It was more for the distraction and so that we did not have to talk. I was wrapped up in my thoughts when the nurse came in to give an update. Jordyn was doing very well, and they were going to be bringing her back in about a half hour. Also, once she was awake, they were going to increase her dietary restrictions to liquids. She would be able to eat broth, Jell-O, and drink juices as well as black coffee.

When the nurse left, I turned to Mark, and we both started laughing. Jordyn was so excited for food, and I could guarantee that this was not what she would call food. She was expecting to be able to have a hamburger or pizza or something solid. Unless we threw those into a blender, she was not going to be allowed to eat any of it.

"We are definitely going to have to get more information on how long these dietary restrictions are going to last. She is going to be a bear!" I said to Mark. "I would think that if they are planning on releasing her by Wednesday, it would have to just be this first meal, or today, and then increase her slowly tomorrow. She has to be able to eat real food by the time that she leaves to ensure that she can tolerate it, right?" I asked, already knowing the answer.

Mark answered, "I would think so. Otherwise, they would have to keep her longer."

That thought had not really crossed my mind, and now I was a little concerned. But the doctor had said he wanted to keep her one extra night just as a precaution.

Michele walked in right about that time. "Good morning. What did I miss? Is surgery over? How did she do?" She was rapid-fire asking questions. Mark and I just stood staring at her. She finally stopped and looked at the two of us. "Are you guys okay? You have not said anything," she asked.

"We were waiting for you to take a breath," I kidded. "Surgery is over. She did well. There was a small issue during surgery where her blood pressure dropped a bit, but she is fine. They just want to keep her one extra night to make sure that there are no aftereffects from it. So it does not look like she will be coming home until Wednesday."

Michele looked a little disappointed.

"Oh, and she has to now be on a liquid diet, although we are not sure how long. We still need to ask the nurse or doctor about how long that will be."

Michele winced. "Oh, no. That is *not* going to make her happy at all. Has anyone told her yet?"

"We have no idea since we have not seen her yet. The nurse just came in to give us the update. She should be back any minute. But I do not want to be the one to tell her."

"Tell her what?" I heard from behind Michele. It was the nurse returning with Jordyn. "Tell me what?" Jordyn repeated.

Mark, Michele, and I exchanged a look. I then walked over and kissed her forehead and looked over her arm that was all bandaged. "That we are very happy that your surgery went well and you were coming back to us." I lied a little just because I did not want to dump that on her right away or, in all honesty, be the one to tell her.

The nurse must have known what we were talking about because while she was walking around the bed plugging in all the monitors, she whispered, "I have not told her about the liquids yet."

I looked at her like someone looks at a dirty child. Then I looked at Mark and nodded toward him mouthing the words "You get to tell her." He shook his head no at me. I looked at Michele, but she was avoiding my gaze.

I looked back toward Jordyn who was trying to help the nurse adjust her in bed so that she could be comfortable. When she finally got into position, she sunk down as if exhausted. I walked over and put my hand on her good arm.

"How are you feeling? Still pretty sleepy?" She nodded. "Well, try to get some sleep now. We can go out for a little while so that you can rest. That was a lot for you after just having had the other surgery. Your body is going to want to do a lot of sleeping. That is when the body heals!" I kissed her on the forehead.

Mark and Michele followed suit, giving her some love, and then we headed out of the door. Once we were in the hallway, we decided to go out and find some food. It was still too early for lunch, but it was beyond the normal breakfast hour. So we decided to go to a coffee shop and just get coffee for the time being.

We had coffee and then decided to just wander around a little. We had all been cooped up since the night of the accident, so it felt good to get out and stretch our legs and feel the sun. It was a bit odd for me as I had not wandered around this area in some time. Some of the stores had changed, but most things were the same.

I was able to get some of my favorite body lotions and got some for Jordyn too. There was nothing worse than being stuck in a hospital bed and not being able to shower or do your normal grooming. I was hoping that just something small might help Jordyn to feel a little more normal. Or at least as much as she possibly could given the circumstances.

I also picked up new pajamas for her. It was a tradition in our family that if you have a surgery, you get new pajamas. With that logic, I really owed her two pairs, so I bought her a second pair. She was probably going to be living in them for the next few weeks anyway while she is healing.

We meandered through a few more shops just browsing, none of us wanting to go back to just sitting in the hospital again. After a few hours, I said that I should probably get back to check on Jordyn. Mark and Michele decided that they were going to go take care of a few things and would come up to the hospital for visiting hours later.

I returned to the hospital to find Daniel in Jordyn's room. She was sleeping, and he was just sitting watching TV next to her bed. He had his hand on her good arm. I stood in the doorway thinking that we had really done something right. Our children were really good people. I was standing there, admiring them when Daniel turned to see me in the doorway.

"Hey, Mom. Why are you standing there looking creepy?" He laughed.

"I just did not want to disturb your moment with your sister!" I walked over and gave him a hug. "How is she? How long have you been here?" I asked, giving Jordyn a kiss on the forehead.

"Just about an hour. She has been sleeping most of the time that I've been here. I did not want to wake her because I know she needs it. She has been through a lot in the past couple of days!" he said as he was looking at her. "She half woke up at one point and tried to turn over, but from the look on her face, it hurt too much, so she went back to sleep. I'm not even sure she knows I'm here," he said, looking up at me.

"I am sure that she does. You kids have always had a sixth sense about each other. You could always tell when one of you was in trouble or needed help. Have the nurses been here since you came in?" I asked.

"I have not seen any yet," Daniel said.

As if on cue, in walked the nurse with her equipment to take vitals. "Sorry, I'm just doing my vitals check," she said as she came into the room.

"Is she due for pain medication yet? She tried moving, and it looked like she was in a good amount of pain," I asked. I was not sure how long ago she had been given any medication, and it was now several hours post-surgery, so any anesthesia and pain medication from that had to have worn off by now.

"She is going to be due here pretty quickly. We could certainly get her something," the nurse said as she set up her equipment. That woke Jordyn.

While she was waking up, she was looking around as if to try to get her bearings. "Hey, kiddo" Daniel said to her. She put her head back down and smiled at him.

"Hey," she squeaked out. "When did you get here?" she asked.

"About an hour or so ago. I was just watching TV waiting for you to wake up. I finally got the remote for once!" he chided with her. She smiled back but then winced. "Does it hurt bad?" Daniel asked.

"I can't decide which hurts more, my arm or my stomach. My arm is still kind of numb from whatever they put in it for the surgery, but it's a deep bone ache, and it really hurts when I move it at all. My stomach is really bad when I move at all," Jordyn said as she tried to wiggle her way to a sitting position, making terrible faces the entire time.

The nurse reached over and tried helping her to sit up using the bed remote. She was able to sit up a little easier but was struggling to get comfortable with the large bandage that was on her arm. Daniel sat next to her looking very helpless and like he wanted to do something but was afraid to hurt her.

He finally asked, "Can I help you to move or move something for you? You look so uncomfortable."

"I honestly don't know what will help. I feel like no matter what I do, I cannot get comfortable," Jordyn said.

The nurse chimed in with, "I can get you some more pain meds. You are just about due anyway. Maybe that will help with the pain enough that you will be able to get comfortable. Let me just take your vitals quick then I will go get them," she said as she slipped the blood pressure cuff onto her arm.

She took Jordyn's vitals twice. After the first time, she looked a little puzzled and waited a couple of minutes and tried it again. She wrote down the information in Jordyn's chart. I wanted to know if there was a problem, especially in light of what happened in the operating room, but since we had not told Daniel or Jordyn yet what had happened, I decided to wait to talk to the nurse when I had her alone.

The nurse left, and Daniel gave me an odd look. He must have seen my face when I was watching the nurse and did not know what was happening. I looked at him as if to say "Not now" and then I told Jordyn that I had gone shopping.

"So when we went out, I wanted to make sure that you got some good sleep, so we wandered around downtown. I found you a few things. First, I got you some awesome body lotion to try to make you feel a little more normal. Hopefully, you will be able to take a shower soon or at least get a good sponge bath." I started to hand her lotion and realized she was one-handed, so I put it on her side table. "Then as is tradition, I got you surgery jammies. And since you had two surgeries, I got you two pairs!" I held them up, and Jordyn smiled.

"I would say that I should do this more often since I needed new pajamas, but this sucks!" She laughed then moaned from the pain.

The nurse came in and gave her the pain medication. While she was there, I asked when Jordyn might be able to take a shower or get a good sponge bath. She said that she would bring the items for a sponge bath but that she would have to see the doctor at least once post-op in order to be able to get the release for a real shower.

As the nurse left, I looked at Jordyn and shrugged. "It's better than nothing! At least you can get cleaned up and feel a little more human."

Daniel and I visited for a little while, and Jordyn continued to nap on and off. It was nice to be able to just visit with him and catch up. We chat often on the phone, but we have not been able to just sit and talk in quite some time. I enjoyed catching up on what was happening with him. I also appreciated the fact that he was interested in how things were going with me and my new life. It was odd to talk to him about it, but it also felt good. I had felt like this other life was so completely separate that I needed to keep it quiet. I never discussed it with Mark or the kids. It just felt odd to talk about it.

Around five, Daniel said that he needed to run as he had an evening class and needed to grab something to eat before. He stood up and kissed his sister on the forehead as she had fallen back to sleep.

Then he came over to say goodbye to me. I stood up and hugged him for a long time. When I stepped back, I said, "Thank you."

"For what?" he asked.

"Thank you for asking me about what is happening with me. I have felt so awkward about talking to any of you about it that it was starting to feel like this taboo, secret life. But for better or worse, it is my life now. So again, thank you for being interested."

"Of course, Mom. It has been weird to talk about because we always thought it would be you and Dad, but things change whether we like it or not. We either have to adapt or get left behind, right?" he said, shrugging shoulders.

"When did you get so smart?" I smiled at him as he headed for the door.

"When I was born!" he called back. "Love you, Mom! Tell Jordyn I will check on her tomorrow."

"I will, love you too," I said as he walked out of the door, again thinking what a great job we had done.

I settled into my chair for a bit and flipped through the channels. I must have dozed because when I awoke, the nurse was taking Jordyn's vitals again. I took the opportunity since Jordyn was sleeping again to ask the nurse about what had happened earlier and why she took them twice.

"When I took them the first time, her blood pressure was very low. So I took it again to make sure that the numbers that I was getting were accurate," she answered.

"And were they?" I asked.

"I did get the same general numbers the second time. Normally, I would have tried on her other arm the second time, but as that was the arm she had surgery on this morning, I did not want to use it."

"So explain to me the numbers and why it was concerning. How low were they?" I asked.

"Well, they were running around 98/58, which is quite a bit lower than we like to see," she said. Then quickly followed that with, "But you have to remember that she has been sleeping a lot, and she did just have surgery."

"Yes, but the doctor said that it had dropped during surgery also. So clearly there is something happening that is outside of the norm. Is something being done to watch this? Can it become a bigger issue? And the bigger question, what is causing it? Obviously, her sleeping a lot and the recent surgery cannot be the only reason it would happen, correct?" I asked.

"We are watching it. As to the causes and other questions, you may want to discuss this with the doctor. He will be making his rounds this evening to follow up after her surgery, so definitely ask him." With that, she packed up her equipment and headed out.

I was pacing when Mark and Michele came in, bringing food. I turned and smiled at them, trying not to let them see that something was up, but Mark knows me too well.

"What is wrong?" he asked.

"Nothing is wrong, you just startled me a little. I was lost in thought, that is all." I gave him the look that said that I will talk to him later about it. So he dropped the subject for the moment.

We ate dinner, and Michele talked a million miles an hour to her sister, mostly just because she was masking her discomfort with being in the hospital. Jordyn was still hooked to several monitors in light of her recent blood pressure issues, and she was still on IV fluids since she could not eat solid foods yet. We tried not to flash our food in her face since she wanted nothing more than to eat, but she did not want us to leave her again. She did get broth and Jell-O for dinner, so she ate with us, pretending that she was eating a hamburger.

Daniel stopped back in like he promised his sister earlier. With all the activity in the room, I took the opportunity to take a walk out to the nurses' station to see if I could get more information on what the plan was or if they had spoken to the doctor yet. I was able to catch the nurse. I told her that I was trying not to worry the rest of my family, but I wanted to get some information on what the doctor's thoughts were on what could be happening with Jordyn and what the plan of treatment was moving forward.

"I was able to talk to the doctor, and he wanted to talk to a couple of other specialists," the nurse said.

I knew that she was not able to make diagnoses or relay any information like that, but her lack of information was extremely frustrating.

"Did he indicate what type of specialist?" I asked. "I would probably expect a cardiologist, but could there be others?" I was not sure that I wanted the answer, but not knowing was killing me too.

"Honestly, he did not say. But he did say that he would be in to speak with you and Jordyn once he had some more information and/or set up a consultation with them." She smiled at me and said, "I have worked with this doctor for years, and I can assure you that he is very thorough and will do everything that he can to make sure she gets the care she needs even if it is not from him. He has a background as a military medic as well as prior emergency room care, so he is very thorough!"

I was relieved to hear that he was not just going to say he did his part and leave us to figure the rest out. However, we were no closer to an answer than we were before.

"Thank you," I said to her. "That does make me feel a little better. Now if we could just get some answers or it would resolve, then I would feel a whole lot better!" I smiled at her.

I turned and headed down the hall back toward Jordyn's room lost in my own thoughts. When I looked up, I saw Mark standing in the hallway.

"Where have you been?" he asked with his arms crossed. "I know something is up. Talk to me, Laura. What's going on?"

"I didn't want to say anything in front of the kids because I don't want them to be worried. Jordyn's blood pressure has been dropping to alarming levels again. They are not sure what is causing it. I just went to the nurses' station to find out what the doctor's thoughts were about what it was or how they are going to treat it. The nurse said that he is consulting with a couple of specialists and he will be in to talk to us once he knows what he is doing next." I paused for him to react.

Mark stood there for a minute as if to take in the information that I had just given him. "So when they said it dropped in surgery from what they thought was just due to having surgery a day before, it could be something else?" He was trying to wrap his head around what I was saying. "When did it drop again?"

"Earlier today when they were taking her vitals while I was out. The nurse said she had to take them twice because it was so low she thought she read them wrong. Then when I came back and she came in to take them, it happened again."

"But none of the other monitors are picking up on anything?" he asked.

"Not that I am aware of," I said. "I have a lot of questions once the doctor comes in. I'm thinking we may need to have a consultation with a cardiologist to find out what is causing the drop. I mean, I would think that it would be a cardiologist because it would have to be heart related, right?" I asked, now questioning whether that was right.

"I am not sure," Mark said. "I believe that it can also be due to undetected bleeding in the body. So maybe there was an injury that they did not previously notice."

Now both of us were running through different scenarios in our minds.

"Okay, we need to stop," I said. "We cannot let the kids know what is going on until we have some answers. I don't want to worry anyone else any more than everyone already is. The doctor will be in to talk to us, and he can give us answers rather than us just speculating on what could be. Agreed?" I looked at Mark.

I really needed his support on this one. We had to be a united front to protect our family and to help all of us get through this. If this was going to be something bigger, we needed to handle it the right way.

"Agreed. We really need to deal with this together and figure out what is happening. Then we can go from there for a solution," Mark said.

We decided to go to the cafeteria to grab coffees so that the kids would not question why we were gone so long. When we got back, the three of them were laughing at something they were remembering from when they were young. Jordyn was doing her best not to laugh and holding her stomach, telling the other two to stop because it hurt. I looked at Mark as if to say "*This* is why we need to keep this to ourselves until we know what is going on."

In my heart, I knew that with the strength of our family, we would get through it together. We just needed to figure out what "it" was.

After a couple of hours had passed, Daniel had left to take Michele home. Mark and I were still sticking around to try to talk to the doctor for some more answers. We had settled in to watch a movie while Jordyn dozed. I heard footsteps coming in the door, and my heart started racing. I knew the doctor's footsteps over the nurses by now. I sat up quickly, causing Mark to look to see what was happening. He saw the expression on my face, so he knew.

I instinctively glanced at Jordyn to see if she was sleeping, looking back at the doctor with a pleading look. He smiled at me and whispered for us to step outside. Once outside of Jordyn's room, I looked at the doctor.

"Thank you. I just don't want to concern her until we have an idea of what is happening. I think I'm scared enough for both of us." I tried to laugh, but it sounded choked. I felt Mark's hand on the small of my back to give assurance that he was there, just as he had done for years.

"I apologize for taking so long to come in to see you. I know that you were asking the nurses for an update. I just wanted to consult with some of my colleagues before I spoke with you about what is happening." He paused to make sure that we were following him. "As you know, Jordyn had a drop in blood pressure while we were in surgery. That does happen from time to time. She just had a traumatic event. Sometimes, just an injury can cause a drop in blood pressure. She had also had a recent surgery. More trauma to her body. Since surgery, the nurses have been documenting ongoing drops in her blood pressure. I want to ensure that there were no other injuries that we have not yet found. I have ordered additional blood work. This will show whether there are any infections in her system, which could cause the low blood pressure. I also want to make sure there is no other bleeding that we missed. We are also going to do a cardiac panel to ensure that there are no underlying conditions that she was not aware of prior to the accident."

He must have seen the look on my face; if it was anything like how I was feeling, it must have appeared as utter terror. He continued, "I have spoken with a cardiology colleague who will be reviewing the results and who will also be consulting and completing an examination just for precautionary measures. I do not want to miss anything. We have her here. I want to be as thorough as possible so that when she leaves here, we can be sure that she will be going home to recover from her current injuries and not dealing with any other problems." He looked from Mark to me. "Are you in agreement with that plan?"

We both nodded our heads. I added "I just want some answers as to what is causing this."

"We may not get an actual answer. However, we will be able to rule other problems out. If the blood work and the cardiac work up are normal and we can rule out cardiac and bleeding issues, we will have to assume that it is her body's reaction to the multiple traumas. That is not to say that we will just drop the subject at that point. We will want to have continued monitoring to ensure that she recovers fully with no residual effects. This is all presuming that the blood work and cardiac work up are normal." He paused to gauge our reactions.

I looked at Mark who nodded at me. "I think we can agree on that plan of action," I said. "I think my biggest concern was additional bleeding or a cardiac issue. But if we can rule both of those things out and that is an otherwise normal reaction that can happen over a trauma, I would be okay with that. How about you, Mark?" I looked at him for a reaction.

"I guess I would just say to start with the testing and go from there." He was looking a little lost and overwhelmed by all this. It had been a lot over the last few days with everything that had happened. Now we have one more blow. I knew that I had said it before, we just needed to get through this.

I looked up and smiled at him and took his hand. "We will get through this."

The doctor looked in the door at Jordyn who was still sleeping. "I will order the blood work now. I am going to have the entirety of the tests completed twice, once tonight and once again in the morning. I just want to ensure the accuracy and make sure that nothing changes over that time. I will also let Dr. Phillips know that he should add her to his rounds for a complete cardiac evaluation once the blood work comes back and he can review it. You should be hearing from him sometime midday tomorrow."

"Can we assume that this means that she will not be released before this is resolved?" I asked.

"I would prefer to keep her here until we have the results back from the examination and the testing, especially in light of the ongoing drop in her blood pressure. That can make her a fall risk. Plus, until we know what is causing it, I want to be able to monitor."

"That makes sense. We will try to explain a little of what is happening to her. I just do not want her worrying any more than she needs to be. She needs to just concentrate on resting and recovering from the surgeries. I think we will just tell her that they are doing some additional testing just to be on the safe side. If we don't find anything, then we have not worried her unnecessarily. If there is something going on, we can go from there." I looked from the doctor to Mark. "Can we agree to that?"

They both agreed. The doctor headed down the hall, advising that he would be back to see her in his normal rounds in the morning and once he had reviewed the blood work from both tonight and the morning. Mark and I stood in the hall just trying to absorb all of it.

I looked at Mark and said, "Well, that was not bad news. It was just uncomfortable news. We still need to figure this out. Once we have a better idea of what it could be, we will just plan our attack from there. In the meantime, she is getting round-the-clock care and monitoring. Personally, I am glad that they are not sending her home. If something happens, I would rather that she was here where they can immediately respond."

Mark nodded his head in agreement.

"We will be fine, we always are," I said, more to convince myself than Mark.

We headed back into Jordyn's room to finish watching our movie although I'm not sure that either of us heard a word of it. We watched the next movie that came on even though neither of us really had any interest. The nurse came in and checked Jordyn's vitals and did the first round of blood work.

Mark and I exchanged a look and I said, "Part one."

We continued to watch the movie while Jordyn dozed on and off. Mark ran downstairs to get us something to eat since neither of us had eaten much all day. I was not really hungry but knew that I would not be any good to anyone if I was worn down. Jordyn woke up at one point and asked why we were still there. Honestly, I did not want to leave her side, and I didn't think Mark really wanted to either. I had not even left to get food because I was afraid to leave her. I also did not want Mark to leave my side, and I think he was feeling the same way.

Mark finally decided to say his goodbyes for the night although reluctantly. He gave me a hug as he was leaving and whispered in my ear "We've got this. I love you" and then he left.

I settled into my chair with a million thoughts running around in my head. Before I knew it, I was waking up to sunlight. I must have been more exhausted than I realized.

Jordyn was awake talking to the nurse who was taking her vitals and more blood work. *Part two*, I thought and grabbed my phone to text Mark. It was not quite 7:00 a.m., and I did not really want to wake him, but I figured if I sent a text, maybe it would not wake him up. He would want to know about this since it was the second piece of the puzzle. A few minutes later, Mark walked in with coffees in hand.

He handed me my coffee. "You are a lifesaver!" I said. "Thank you."

Then he walked over to Jordyn, kissed her on the forehead, and handed her a hot chocolate. He looked at the nurse who had come back to give Jordyn her morning medications. "She can have hot chocolate, right? I assumed that since it was liquid, she could drink it."

The nurse looked at him and smiled. "Of course. We may actually move her to more solid foods today."

"Yesssss!" Jordyn shrieked. "I am *starving*!"

Everyone laughed. It definitely sounded like she was feeling better.

Then I started wondering if that could have something to do with her blood pressure dropping too. Maybe the lack of food was contributing. The more I thought about it, the more I was feeling like this all may be fine after all. Between the trauma, the back-to-back surgeries, the lack of food, and just the entire situation, it would make sense that her blood pressure could drop. Plus, she had lost blood when she had the bleed. I was feeling less scared the more I analyzed all of it. Now I just needed the test results to confirm my theory. I prayed that would be the case.

We all sat sipping our morning drinks when the doctor popped his head in. "How is everyone this morning?" he asked.

I was a little surprised that he was in so early. There was no way that the results were back from this morning's blood draw that fast. I started to panic a bit as that must mean that last night's tests showed something bad. I looked at him with pleading eyes, trying to keep my voice calm.

"We are good doctor, how are you?" I kept thinking, *Please do not give us bad news.*

"I'm good. I just had a couple of extra minutes on my early morning rounds, and I heard you all talking in here. I just wanted to pop my head in and check on my favorite patient," he said to Jordyn. "How are you feeling this morning? Now that the anesthesia and the injected numbing is all worn off, any severe pain or other concerns?" he said as he looked at the bandages on her arm.

"No, I'm actually feeling pretty good. I can definitely tell that something happened, but it is not terrible. I will be better when I can have real food again." She looked at him as if to get confirmation that it was going to happen.

The doctor smiled at her and said, "Well, I have good news. I think that we can start you back on solid food today. I still want you to take it easy. No jumping into heavy meals. Light things only, like chicken noodle soup, cottage cheese, pudding, or those types of consistency. You need to allow your system to build back up before you chow down on a burger." He laughed.

"I guess that is better than nothing," said Jordyn.

"If you do alright with those foods today, maybe tomorrow you can get your burger." He smiled at her.

"Sweet," she said. "Thank you."

"Do any of you have any questions for me?" He looked at each of us.

I looked at Mark and at Jordyn then said, "No, I think we are set for now."

"Okay, well, then I will see you later on my normal rounds. I want to look at the notes from the nurses, and I will check back in for my formal evaluation." He stood up and smiled at us. "Have a good morning."

As he left the room, Jordyn looked at Mark and I and said, "Okay, you two, what is your problem?"

I looked at her trying to act completely shocked and as if I had no idea what she meant. "What are you talking about? What did we do?" I asked.

"When he came in, you two looked like you just saw a ghost. What is going on? Are you not telling me something? Am I dying?" She started to look scared.

"Oh, honey, no! I have no idea what you mean! I was just not expecting to see him this early. He caught me off guard before I got my coffee in, that is all." I looked at Mark as if to ask for his help.

He piped in with "I don't think I looked like anything. I was not expecting to see him, so maybe that was my face. But nothing more." He smiled at her.

She looked at each of us and said, "Fine, but if I'm dying and you are not telling me, I'm coming back to haunt you both!"

We all laughed while secretly those words stung because we still had no idea what was happening.

I excused myself to freshen up and get dressed. It was really to regain my composure. It was not fair that we were not giving Jordyn the truth about what was going on. Technically, she was an adult, but with everything that she had been through in the last few days, I felt a deep need to protect her in any way that I could. Mark and I were already doing enough worrying for all three of us. We really just wanted her to spend her energy healing right now. We were all still hopeful that it was nothing to be worried about, so there was no need to worry her unnecessarily about it.

The nurse came in and did her morning vitals check and also drew blood for the final labs that the doctor would need for more information. I was secretly hoping that this would be the final piece that would put everything together so we could have an answer as to what was happening. We needed to be able to move on from this in order to start the process of Jordyn's healing and getting back to normal…whatever that means!

Michele made a quick visit with coffee for all. This was definitely welcome although I already was crawling out of my skin waiting for the doctor to come in with answers. I was not sure that I really needed more caffeine.

Sometime late morning, the doctor finally made a stop in to see Jordyn again. He smiled at us when he came in. "Good morning again! How is everyone doing?"

We all looked at him, Mark and I exchanging looks as if to say "Here we go." I tried to pretend that I was not bursting at the seams for an answer.

"We are all doing well. Good to see you again!"

"Well, I have good news. Everything looks good with your blood work, and your vitals have been okay. I would like to see your blood pressure a little higher than it has been. However," he looked at Mark and I as if he was answering our unspoken question and emphasized, "drops in blood pressure can happen after a trauma especially where you had the accident, then the bleed that required the surgery, then a second surgery, all in just three days' time. Not to mention the amount of pain that you have been in. Your blood work does not show any signs of infection or blood loss, but given the reduced blood pressure and the trauma, I would like to have an ultrasound of your abdomen completed just so that we can be completely certain that it is not another underlying condition. If that is clear, then I do not see any reason that you would not be able to resume eating regular foods again and possibly go home tomorrow. I do just want to monitor you for a few more vitals and, of course, that ultrasound. How does that sound?" He looked at Jordyn who was already grinning from ear to ear.

"That sounds amazing! I cannot wait to have real food. I do have to ask though, how low was my blood pressure to be of concern?"

"It has been staying fairly low in the not-dangerous zone but in the zone where we were concerned enough to need to watch it and make sure that it was not the sign of something more. That is usually our indicator that there could be blood loss somewhere. But it can be caused from stress, pain, trauma, among other things. You have had all of those three, so likely that is the contributing factor. However, we really just wanted to make sure that we ruled out the other more serious possibilities before taking a wait-and-see stance. If the ultrasound results are normal, we can increase your salt intake a little as well as your fluid intake, and that should stabilize it into the normal range. I don't think there is anything to worry about at all." He smiled at Jordyn and glanced at Mark and I. "Do any of you have any questions?"

We all shook our heads no.

"Well, then I will get you moving down to ultrasound and order a regular diet with the expectation that those results are normal. If not, I will be back in to discuss what we found. Otherwise, I will check back in with you all this evening." With that, he headed toward the door.

"Thank you, Doctor," I called after him. He turned and smiled and then walked out.

"So you guys knew the whole time that there was something of concern, didn't you?" Jordyn looked at Mark and me. "Why didn't you just tell me if it was not that big of a deal?" she asked.

"We were not sure it was not a big deal yet. Your blood pressure dropped during both surgeries and stayed uncomfortably low. They have been monitoring it very closely to make sure that you did not bottom out or crash. We just did not know what was causing it yet. You have been through so much in the last few days that we really did not want you to worry until we had an idea of what was causing it or whether it was serious. We thought if you could rest and heal, it would be better for you in the long run." I stood up and walked toward Jordyn, placing my hand on her good arm. "Besides, you heard the doctor. Stress can cause this to happen as well. So in combination with all the other factors, you did not need the added stress of not knowing what was causing your blood pressure to drop."

"I wonder if that is why I feel so tired. I mean, I know that I just had an accident followed by two surgeries and that I'm on pain meds, but I am just so tired. I feel like I just want to sleep all the time even after a cup of coffee!"

"I would think that could be a symptom, but we can certainly ask. I'm sure that you being stuck in that bed for the last three days when you are normally never stationary for more than a few minutes could have something to do with it too." I laughed.

Mark stepped forward and said, "My mother had an issue with low blood pressure. It was only in certain situations, and the doctors told her it would never be a problem unless it dipped too low. They told her just to eat a bag of chips if she was feeling tired. She used that excuse for years!" He laughed.

Jordyn laughed and said, "I am going to have to remember that excuse the next time I'm teased for eating junk food. I can just say that I'm doing it for my heart!"

Later that day, the doctor came in for his rounds and confirmed that the test results were normal, the ultrasound was normal, and he had confirmed with a cardiologist colleague that given all the factors, it sounded as if it was just stress and trauma related. However, he did want her to follow up with her primary care doctor in a month just for a recheck and suggested that as she was recovering at home, we might just want to check her blood pressure once in a while.

Jordyn just wanted to know if she could eat real food so she could order DoorDash. The doctor was barely out the door before she was on her phone ordering a cheeseburger and fries.

Jordyn was scheduled to be released the next morning, so now I needed to come up with a game plan as to what I was going to do now. She would need to be home, recovering for several weeks. She had significant restrictions on lifting, bending, and no lifting for both the abdominal surgery and her arm. She was also still pretty bruised and sore from the overall accident. I was not willing to just go home and let Mark take care of her. I knew that he could do a good job, but he was not Mom. I needed to be there to see that everything was going well and she was recovering properly.

We were sitting in Jordyn's room, watching a movie and munching on her food order. I was trying to figure out how I was going to handle things with work and whether I was going to stay at the house or get a room nearby.

Mark must have been watching me thinking. He leaned over and whispered, "You can just stay at the house in the guest room. We will get her home tomorrow and just figure it out day by day." He stopped to look at my reaction to make sure that we were on the same page. "Stop trying to plan it all out, Laura. You do not need to have all the answers right now. We can just figure it out as we go. Whatever you need, we can make it happen." He smiled at me and leaned back into his chair.

I always appreciated Mark's insight into a situation. He had a way of making me feel like I could stop and just take things one step at a time. I always felt like I had to have it all figured out even when figuring it all out was so outrageous. His perspective of step-by-step just seemed so much smarter and less complicated yet somehow irresponsible. I was brought up that if you did not have a plan, you were doomed. I needed to always know the next step. I could not just wing it.

However, in this instance, I needed to just take it step-by-step. There was no way to know how quickly Jordyn was going to heal. It could be very different from day to day, so I would have to just allow her healing to take the lead. I can just figure it out as I go. I would call my office and try to work from home for a while so that I could stay with her until she was able to take care of herself. She would need help just to do normal daily activities, like dressing and showering for instance.

Later that evening, as Mark was leaving, I offered to walk him out. When we got out to the hallway, I stopped and looked at him.

"Thank you. I know that it is going to be awkward having me at the house. I really do appreciate you letting me stay and take care of her." I smiled at him and stepped forward to hug him.

Mark hugged me back, saying, "You don't need to thank me. It is our daughter and our home. I would not expect you to want to be anywhere else, and I would never stop you from being with her." He stepped back and smiled at me. "Plus, I am selfishly happy that you will be home. I really miss you, Laura. As difficult as the last few days have been, I have loved having you here with me…with us. We all miss you, so it will be good to have you home." He stepped forward and kissed me on the forehead. "Have a good night. I will see you in the morning." Then he turned and walked down the hall to the exit.

I watched him leave and stood in the hall just a little longer. I was sad to see him leave. I had become very comfortable having him around and hated it when he left in the evening. I turned and walked back into Jordyn's room.

"He's not wrong, you know," Jordyn turned and said to me. "We really miss you, Mom!" She teared up a little as she said it.

I walked over to her bed and laid my hand on her arm. "I know, baby, I'm sorry. It's just so complicated now." I was fighting back tears myself.

"What is complicated, Mom? You love Dad. It is so obvious. We all miss you. Do you want to come home?" Jordyn looked at me as if pleading for an answer.

"I do, but I have…I…" My voice trailed off. I what? What did I have that was keeping me from just going home? My job? My apartment? My what? I honestly had nothing that was so important in my life that I could not just pack up and move home. It was easy enough to just pack up and leave everything in my life that was extremely important, so why could I not just make this move? I honestly could not give myself or Jordyn an answer. Something was holding me in place. I could not give an answer.

"I don't know, Jordyn. I have no idea why I cannot bring myself to just uproot and move home. I cannot give you a good reason at all." I started to cry. It was the kind of cry that was unproportional for the situation, but it was the buildup of months of not crying or months of holding in my emotions. It was the loss, the fear, the frustration, the doubt, the missing my family, my home, my normal. All of it flooded out of me like a tidal wave of emotion.

After I was finally able to regain my composure, I looked at Jordyn. "I am so sorry! I don't know where that came from! I think it was just the last few days and lack of sleep. I need to just let it all out!" I joked. "I think I'm better now! You should try it. It is very invigorating." I laughed, trying to make light of the fact that I just completely broke down standing in my daughter's hospital room after everything that she had been through as if my problems were worse.

"Mom, you can break down anytime you want or need to! I remember plenty of times that I broke down to you over stupid things. We all need to from time to time. You have been through a lot. We all have. You do not always need to be strong for everyone." She smiled at me. "But you do need to figure out what you want and what is going to make you happy. I know Dad misses you terribly. He pretends that everything is great, but he is not. And it is obvious that you are not either. It sounds like you need to take some time together and figure things out." She paused and looked out the window. "Maybe this accident was just what the family needed to get back to where we should be!" She turned back and smiled at me. "Although I would have rather not have been stuck here." She motioned around her room. Then we both laughed.

"How did you get so smart?" I asked, hugging her as gently as I could.

"I learned from the best," she said as she tried to hug me with one arm and a sore belly.

We settled in for the night knowing that in the morning we would be preparing her to head home and I would be starting my new journey. I really needed to do some deep thinking and decide what I wanted to do moving forward. I also needed to figure out what was stopping me from just going home. I think I needed to start with figuring out why I left in the first place and go from there. But there was plenty of time for that while I was helping Jordyn to get back on her feet. It was time for all of us to do some healing.

Getting Jordyn discharged, into the car, and home was more work than I had expected. It was easy to forget that she had been in a traumatic car accident and was not particularly mobile with her lying in a hospital bed looking and acting fairly normal. When she stood up to get into the car once we had wheeled her in her wheelchair down to meet us, it caused her to turn ghostly white and nearly pass out. She had not stood up for several days other than to walk to the bathroom and back, which was not often.

By the time that we got her home, she was on the brink of collapsing from exhaustion and pain. She had been given her pain medication before we left the hospital, but it was given by mouth which did not always have the same effect as an IV medication. It took all her strength, and mine, to get her out of the car and in the front door. Mark was waiting for us and was able to take over helping to transport her up to her room. I followed along, making sure that they did not fall down the stairs and ran in to make sure that her bed was ready for her when she went to sit down.

It was a very different feeling going from a mobile hospital bed with round-the-clock care to being home with a flat bed and yelling when you need something. I wanted to make sure that she had everything that she needed within arm's reach so that she did not have to stand up or stretch for anything if we were not right there. She needed to be able to concentrate on healing and resting to get better. Of course, it was not just her arm, but she had also had a significant abdominal surgery, so recovery was going to be slow and painful.

We set her up in her room, made sure she had something to drink, and then left so that she could go to sleep. She was exhausted from the trip, and emotionally, it was rough being that it was the first time she had been home since she left to go to the movies several days ago.

We walked downstairs, and Mark headed to the kitchen. I sat down at the table, tired both mentally and physically. Mark must have read my mind because he brought me a glass of wine and sat at the table next to me. "I say that we all take this evening to just settle in and enjoy not needing to run to and from the hospital. I will make us some dinner, and we can settle in to watch a movie. Jordyn will be sleeping for a while, and we could all use the down time!"

He looked at me and smiled, reaching over to place his hand on top of mine. "You look exhausted. Why don't you go take a real shower and get comfortable. I will start making us some dinner. Michele should be back shortly, so we can fight over what movie to watch." He laughed just looking at me as if he was studying me.

I could not argue with any of that. I was exhausted, and the entirety of the last several days was starting to settle into my bones. I had been showering at the hospital and never feeling quite human while sleeping and staying there. "I think that all sounds wonderful! I am willing to start a movie, but I cannot guarantee how much of it I will see. After this glass of wine, a hot shower with real soap and shampoo, and then a decent meal, I will be sleeping before you know it!" I laughed.

I was grateful in this moment that he knew me so well and I was comfortable enough to be able to just let go of this entire ordeal and move forward. I was hoping that a good, hot shower washing off the smell of the hospital would also wash away the stress of what we had been through.

I sat smiling at Mark for a few minutes, allowing him to leave his hand on mine. "Thank you," I said. "Thank you for being you and knowing exactly what I need right now. I am glad that we have moved past all of the stress and drama of the last few days and that we are on to the healing process. I know it will not be easy, but like everything else, we can get through this."

Mark smiled back, saying, "Together!"

"Together!" I responded.

Then I raised my glass as if to toast that sentiment and took a long slow sip. The sweet taste and tang slowly slid down my throat, and I envisioned it being the peace that I had been searching for. I was taking it in and savoring it. I stood up and said, "I am going to go try to wash off the hospital smell and maybe cry out all the emotions I have been bottling up now that we are on the uphill swing." I smiled, heading down the hallway to my room to gather my clothes and head to the shower.

Crying was exactly what I did. With my face under the water and just allowing myself to relax entirely, I cried. I cried for the events of the last few days and the accident that could have been so much worse and could have taken almost my entire family at once. I cried for the terror of Jordyn's blood pressure issues that nearly made her code on the operating table twice. I cried for the confusion that was still in my head over being here, with Mark, and for hurting him so deeply by leaving. I cried because my heart was telling me to just come home, but something was still stopping me. Right here, right now, in this moment, it was the closest that I had been to walking away from my new life and just coming home. Then I realized that I was home. This was my home. Not this house, not these four walls, but here, with my family. With Mark, this was home.

I expected that the move, after so many years of the same thing, would be scary and different. But for the first time in months, since even before I walked out the door with all my belongings, I felt like I was home. I felt like I was where I belonged. I was not sure if it was because of what we had all just gone through and the release of all that emotionally, so I was not willing to act on my feelings quite yet. I wanted to get a good night's sleep, enjoy the company of my family watching a movie, having a good home-cooked meal, and be in the moment. I will make more permanent decisions later.

When I came downstairs, feeling like a human again, Michele had come home. She hugged me tighter than she had since she was little and scared of thunderstorms. She looked at me and said, "I'm glad you're home, Mom!" I kissed her on the forehead and smiled.

We all agreed on a movie, which was extremely rare and only meant that we were all too tired to argue. I checked on Jordyn for what felt like the twentieth time to make sure that she was sleeping and did not need anything. I had set alarms on my phone to ensure that we were on time with her pain medication so there would be no lapse, causing any increase in pain. We would certainly adjust that as time progressed, but given the fact that she was just home without the ability to have IV medications that worked quicker, we needed to stay on top of her medications.

Dinner was delicious, and just as I had predicted, I had fallen asleep on the couch within minutes of the start of the movie. I woke up as the credits were rolling. Michele had gone to bed, and Mark was cleaning up. I dozed on and off for a few minutes longer. I awoke to Mark standing over me telling me to go to bed. I stood up and headed up the stairs. Then the next thing that I knew, Mark was standing in the doorway of our old room, looking at me lying on our bed. I sat up, looked around, and was completely confused by what I was seeing.

"I…I…I'm sorry, I don't…," I stammered as I stood up and started walking out of the room. Mark stopped me at the door.

"Laura, you don't ever have to apologize or feel bad if you want to come back home…come back to me." He looked in my eyes as if pleading.

I stood there just staring at him, still a little dazed and uncertain about how I had come to be standing in our old room.

"I can see that you are still half sleeping." He smiled. "You were probably just half asleep, and old habits die hard. Especially when you are not fully functioning." He was trying to make sense of the situation for me. He looked at me again and said, "Do you want me to walk you to your room to make sure you get to the right place this time?" Then he chuckled.

"No, I think I can find it," I said, still a little confused and feeling very awkward at this point. "I'm sorry. Good night," I said as I squeezed past him to head down the hall.

"Good night," he said without turning around. I could hear him wait a minute before continuing into the bedroom and closing the door.

I walked into my room, closed the door, and climbed into bed. What made me go there? Maybe Mark was right, and it was just a habit. Or it was something in my brain just acting out what I had been thinking earlier in the shower. Either way, this was not the way to start my first night here. I fell asleep thinking about the possibilities if I had just stayed in there and told him to join me. I certainly would not have minded sleeping next to him again. I missed him holding me at night when I was falling asleep. There was something about his smell and the feeling of protection I had with him by my side.

The next morning, I awoke thinking about the night before. It took a few minutes to realize that I was sleeping alone in the guest room. Unfortunately, I also realized that I would have to face Mark this morning. I was not ready to have any conversation about what that may have meant.

I took my time getting ready and headed down the hall to check on Jordyn. She was awake and already had her morning pain medications as well as her first coffee. We chatted for a few minutes, but I could not put off the inevitable any longer. I headed down the stairs to the kitchen with the rest of the family.

"Well, good morning, sleepyhead!" Mark called over his shoulder from the stove. "I was not sure if I should be making breakfast or brunch!" He joked.

"I guess I was more tired than I thought I was. Although I did warn you about the movie!" I tried to avoid the topic of the rest of the evening. Before he could add anything to my statement, I said, "Wow, that smells good. What are you cooking?"

"I saw this Texas french toast recipe on a video, and it looked amazing. I figured I would try it out on everyone. Since this is Jordyn's first breakfast home, I thought it would be something special for her." Mark spun around with a heaping plate of thick french toast that smelled like a combination of cinnamon and maple.

"Well," I said, "if it tastes anything like it smells, it should be fabulous!"

I stepped past Mark to grab a cup of coffee that I was in desperate need of at this point. As I brushed past him, Mark smiled at me. Now I was questioning whether that was a smile about last night or if it was just his normal smile. I really needed to just stop overthinking this situation. It was really nothing. I went to the wrong room but was only there for minutes before I realized it and moved. It was not like anything had happened between us. Why was I making such a big deal out of it? If I just stopped thinking about it and acted like it never happened, then I would be fine.

I grabbed my coffee and went to sit at the table. Jordyn walked in and surprised all of us. "What are you doing up?" we all asked in unison.

"I am sick of lying in bed. As long as I don't do any lifting, laughing, or coughing, I can at least get up and move around the house. I was hoping to have breakfast with everyone and not feel like a total invalid anymore." She chuckled, wincing a bit.

I jumped up to make sure that she was okay. Jordyn held her hand up as if to stop me. "I'm fine, Mom, really." She sat down and adjusted herself to get comfortable. Between her arm and her abdomen, she was having a tough time getting adjusted.

I could tell that she was getting frustrated, and it was tough for me to watch as a mother. My natural instinct was to help. I gave it a couple of minutes and finally said, "Can I help you?"

She stopped and put her head down. "I was trying not to be so needy, but I do really need help." She was on the verge of tears.

"Honey, you have been home less than twenty-four hours after a significant accident and three days in the hospital. Not to mention two surgeries and two days with no solid food! You need to accept the help for a little while. It's going to take time for your body to heal enough that you can do things on your own again!" I stood up, helped her adjust, and got her another cup of coffee.

"Thanks, Mom. I just hate not being able to do things on my own." She smiled back at me.

"Oh, don't we know that!" Mark chimed in. "Do you remember the time that she refused to let us get her ready for her first soccer game?" He looked at me and laughed. "You were so adamant that you could do it yourself and did not need our help that you had your shin guards over your socks, your cleats were on the wrong feet, and your shorts were backwards."

"That's right," I joined in. "When we asked if we could help and tried to tell you what was wrong, you got so upset that you cried and ran to hide in the car. We had no choice but to let you go to your game like that."

"Yeah, and when your teammates saw you, you just said 'Yeah, well, I like it this way' and walked off to play." I looked at Jordyn who was now laughing and trying to hold her stomach with her good arm.

"I know, and I was absolutely mortified. I swore that I was going to quit and never come back to soccer because I was so embarrassed. But when everyone dropped the subject, it was like it never happened, so I always felt like I could do whatever I wanted on my own. Until now that is." She looked down at her arm.

"Honey, your mother is right. This is a temporary thing. It is all still pretty fresh. Once you start healing, you will get more independence daily. Just look at how far you've come since your first surgery. At least now you were able to get out of bed by yourself and you even made it all the way downstairs. That's progress!" He smiled at her as he sat down at the table.

"Baby steps! Let's learn to crawl before we walk this time!" I laughed, remembering her when she took her first step. She stood up, put her foot out, and ran three steps before falling. She was never one to take things slow. Something I always envied. I was overly cautious and took everything too slow. Not to mention I overthought everything.

My face must have changed because when I looked up, everyone was staring at me. "What? Do I have something on my face?" I asked, knowing it was probably my expression that changed. I really needed to keep my thoughts in check until I was alone.

The rest of the day was pretty uneventful. Mark and Michele ran out to grab some groceries after we made a menu for the rest of the week and a list for the store. I worked with Jordyn to get her set up so that she could have a specific seat in the family room that was easy to access for her for the time being. I was trying to give her some independence so that she did not get so down on herself but reminding her that she would continue to have some limitations that she would just need to accept for the time being.

While we were in her room rearranging some of her things to make it easier for her to do more on her own, she offhandedly asked, "So do you think that you will just stay this time?"

I was taken off guard and stopped what I was doing for a second to think about her question. "Well," I responded, "I do still have a job and an apartment that I need to take care of, so the chances are pretty good that I will need to leave." I wanted to add that I wanted it to be a temporary trip and that I was really hoping to be able to come home, but I had not discussed anything with Mark yet, so he really needed to be the first person that I discussed this with.

"Mom! I don't understand why you have not come home yet! You and Dad obviously still love each other!"

"Baby, love was never the problem. I'm pretty sure that we have loved each other since the day we met. There are just a lot of other factors. Besides, this is really a conversation that I should be having with your father."

"What conversation should you be having with me?" Mark asked, now standing in the doorway.

I spun around, knocking the clothes pile I had just moved onto the floor. I had not heard him come into the house and did not know he had heard any of our conversation.

I stammered, not wanting to have this conversation with him at this moment or with an audience. "Oh, ummmm...Jordyn was just asking—"

"I asked if she was staying for good this time," Jordyn quickly interjected.

I spun around to look at her, but before I could open my mouth to tell her that this was not appropriate, Mark spoke up.

"Jordyn, this is a conversation that Mom and I should be having. I know that you want her home as do I. We all do!" he said, looking at me and smiling. Then he turned back to her and said, "But can we not put her on the spot like this?" Then he smiled that sheepish-boy grin that he gets and looked at me, saying, "Besides, she won't be able to resist my charms...or my cooking for much longer!" Then he chuckled and headed back downstairs, calling out, "I'm going to be starting dinner soon!"

I turned to pick up the clothes I had knocked onto the floor. Jordyn sat for a minute then said, "I'm sorry, Mom. I didn't mean to make that awkward. I was hoping that Dad would side with me and we would be able to convince you to come home. It just does not feel like home without you."

"I know, baby. Believe me, I have thought a lot about it, and a big part of me does want to come home. There are just so many other factors involved now. Plus, I have not discussed any of this with your father. I really think that needs to be the first discussion I have before I make any kind of plans. That is if I were to make any plans." I smiled at her. "I love you all so very much, but this is a huge decision, and it needs to be made together."

"I know, Mom. We all just really want you home." She hugged me with her one good arm. "So do you think you could have that discussion soon?" She laughed. "Is tonight too soon?"

We both laughed. But there was a part of me that was thinking about what she had said. I did not know why I was waiting to talk to Mark. I did know that the longer that I waited, the harder it became to start the conversation. I was hoping that this would make that happen a little easier and smoother now. Although I still was not sure what I was going to say. I didn't feel like I needed to ask permission, and yet in some sense, I felt like I should. I had walked out. I made the decision unilaterally to just leave. I needed to make a joint decision to come home. I also still needed to figure out what I was going to do with the new life I had built. Part of me did not want to give that up. Just like Jordyn, I was feeling very independent, and I was enjoying that aspect of it. As lonely as it was, it was my life, and I had full control. I was also still a little foggy on what pushed me to the decision to leave in the first place. I knew that I had been unhappy, but why?

Mark and I had a great relationship. He was kind, loving, maybe not always there, but neither of us were with everything else this family was involved in, so that was due to situational factors. I knew that I was overwhelmed and that I felt as if I was handling everything. After the last couple of days, I am starting to realize that much of that was my own doing. No one was expecting me to take on everything. It had become part of who I was as a person. I felt like I needed to be in total control of every situation all the time or I am not comfortable. That was something that I needed to work on personally. I never should have punished Mark or the kids for my shortcomings.

Now the issue was going to be whether I could bring myself to return home. That would require acknowledging my failure and my mistake in leaving in the first place. It would also require me to mend what I had broken in my relationships with Mark and with the kids. I know that they were all asking me to come home. I could not help but to wonder if they really expected that I would or if it was just something that they continued to say but did not think would ever happen. I caused a lot of pain for Mark when I walked out. I would need to repair that first if we were to have any hope of fixing our relationship. I was just not sure where to start.

After dinner and cleaning up, we decided on another family movie night. I worked hard on not falling asleep again because I did not want a repeat of last night's fiasco with going to the wrong room. During the movie, we paused it so that the girls could run to the kitchen for after dinner snacks. Mark casually glanced over at me. I gave him a quizzical look.

He chuckled back. "I was just checking to see if you had fallen asleep. I wondered if I would be finding you in my room again tonight." Then he laughed and turned to look at me again. I turned red from embarrassment, and he smiled and said, "Don't be embarrassed. I was not complaining at all!"

The girls walked back into the room before I could answer, so I just gave him a look as if to say stop. He smiled and turned to the girls. "Okay, are we ready now? Before Mom falls asleep?" And with that, he restarted the movie. Now I was determined to stay awake through the whole movie.

After the movie was over, the girls headed to bed, with Michele helping Jordyn to make sure that she was all set for the night. Mark and I picked up the family room and took all the snacks and drinks to the kitchen. As we were setting up coffee for the morning and filling the dishwasher to start it, Mark casually said, "You know, it would not be such a crazy idea if you were to just move home and stay for good."

I stopped filling the coffeepot and paused for a second. I had not rehearsed what I was going to say to him, so I was not prepared to have this discussion yet. "Mark, I—"

Mark interrupted me. "Laura, you do not have to say anything right now. I'm just saying it would not be such a crazy idea. The girls and I miss you, and it has been so great to have you here these last few days." Then he turned to me and looked me in the eye. "I miss you, Laura. I miss you being with me, lying next to me, waking up with me. I miss you."

I started to cry. "Mark, I am so, so sorry!" I was crying so hard that I had a hard time talking. He walked over and put his arms around me and just let me cry.

After several minutes, he stepped back from me and asked, "What are you sorry for, Laura? Is there someone else? You don't want me or love me anymore? What is it that you are sorry for? It's me! You can tell me anything." He looked so broken, and it was my fault.

That thought made me cry harder as I was shaking my head. "No!" I was able to squeak out. Mark immediately recoiled like I had hit him.

"No, you don't love me or want me anymore?"

"Oh god no! That is not what I meant." I stepped toward him. "No, there is no one else. I am sorry for what I have put you and the girls through these last few months. I am sorry for hurting you. I am sorry that I broke us and our family. I am sorry that I could not fix myself, and in trying to, I broke everything that I love. I am so, so sorry!"

Mark reached out, and we hugged for what seemed like hours.

Mark quietly asked again, "Will you come home?"

I did not answer right away. I was trying to find the words to explain what I was feeling. I wanted nothing more than to have all this back, but I did not want to lose myself again in the process. "Mark, I left for a reason. Until I am able to figure that out and fix what is broken with me, I am afraid to come back."

Mark took a deep breath and asked, "Was it me? Is it something that I did or that I do?"

"No," I answered quickly. "No. I do want to talk about all of this, but I need to make sense of it myself in order to explain it to you. I just do not want to jump right back into coming home and go back to our normal routine without fixing it. I do not ever want to be in this place again, so I need to figure out how to fix it." I looked up at him. "Does that make sense?"

He looked down at me with his beautiful, kind, brown eyes and smiled. "Oddly, it makes perfect sense. What if we were to date again? What if we were to stay as things are right now with you in your room and me in mine and we just start dating all over again? That will give you the time and space that you need to figure yourself out, and it will still keep you close to me. Would that work for you?"

I thought for a minute and said, "That actually sounds nice! While I'm here helping Jordyn rehabilitate, we can do just that."

Mark took a step back and held my arms. "What do you mean while you help Jordyn rehabilitate? Are you planning to go back there?" He looked confused and hurt again.

"Mark, I do have commitments there that I cannot just walk away from and not resolve. I have a lease and a job."

"And you have a husband, children, a house, and had a job here that you were able to just walk away from. I do not understand how anything there is more important than that!" He turned and walked to the other side of the kitchen.

He was not wrong, and it was not easy to explain to him as I did not entirely understand my rationale. However, at this moment, I felt like I was being pressured into doing things his way, and that was not how I was going to resolve any of this.

"I know you do not understand, and I promise that I will explain everything as I am able to express it, but I cannot just walk away and jump back to all of this," I said as I motioned around the kitchen. "I love you all more than life itself, but I lost myself in loving you and taking care of you and the firm and all the kids' interests. I needed to take a step back and find myself again. I am no good to anyone as a robot who just does what she needs to do. I am no good to us." I stepped toward him. "I know it makes no sense. I honestly thought that when I left I was going to lose everything, that you would never want me back. That was not what I wanted, but I was at the breaking point, and I had to leave to save myself. If this, if getting us back is an option, I need to do it in a way that I am able to find myself again and be happy, or I will be no good to you or anyone else in this family. Please understand. I love you, and I want to fix things so that we can have our happily ever after."

Mark looked at me for what seemed like forever. Then he said, "I do not understand." He reached out and touched the side of my face. "But I would wait forever for you. So whatever you need to do, I will be here."

I stepped forward into his arms, and the relief was overwhelming. I had been wanting and dreading this conversation. When I walked out that door all those months ago, I never imagined being back here, in his arms, with the expectation of eventually being back to our normal family. I just did not know where to go from here.

"Let's not tell the kids anything," I said, still wrapped in Mark's arms. "I do not want to give them any expectations or have them pressuring me for a timeline that I cannot give them. But I will take you up on dating again. We can take it slow and get back to what we had. We can let them know that we are trying and leave it at that."

"I am okay with that for the time being. It is our relationship, and they need to respect that part. But I think you are going to have more questions around when you are going to come home for them. I will leave that to you."

We stood there hugging for a little longer. Then I stepped back and looked at him. As much as I wanted to follow him up to our room, we needed to go slow with reconnecting, and I needed to be the one to set the pace. Besides, the girls were in the house, and I did not want to give them any wrong ideas. I was going to need to go back to my place at some point even if it was to wrap things up to come home. So it needed to look as if we were staying the course for the time being.

"It is getting late, and you have to be in the office tomorrow, don't you?" I asked. He nodded his head but did not move. I would have to be the first to react, or this was going to go sideways fast.

"Well, good night. I will see you in the morning." I headed toward the stairs.

"Laura," Mark called out. I stopped but did not turn around. I was afraid to, knowing that I was already struggling to go to my own room. "I love you!" he said from behind me.

I turned and looked at him. "I love you too, Mark! Good night!" I turned and went up to my room, quickly closing the door behind me before I changed my mind.

It took a while for me to fall asleep as my head was spinning with our conversation and trying to make sense of things. I had left for a reason that seemed so urgent and important just a few months ago. Now, being here with Mark and the kids, I was struggling to remember that reason. Could it have been as simple as I was just exhausted by my life? The practices and school events, work, taking care of the house with laundry, cooking, and shopping, or was it more? I know that Mark and I seemed to be living our separate lives together. We were always going separate ways but for the same cause, the family. It did not make sense that so close to the finish line of raising our children, I would just leave. It was about to get so much quieter in the house, so why walk away from that? After everything that had happened, I could not remember the reasons.

The next morning, after I awoke, I did not jump right out of bed. My head was still spinning from the night before. I needed time to think, but I was having a tough time doing that when I was completely submerged in the situation. Thinking on it a little more, wasn't that the whole point of this? I made a decision to leave when I was entirely submerged in this life. Apart from this, I was like a blank slate. I was doing my day-to-day routine, getting up, drinking my coffee, going to work, then coming home to an empty house. There was no extra, no one there to share anything with, and there was no substance. Here, in this house, with my family, my life had substance. I had a purpose and my life had meaning. I knew it sounded so cliché, but it truly did.

So how can the thing that gave my life meaning and purpose be the same thing that caused such turmoil within me? What was it that had changed? I remember the entire time I was growing up that

I had wanted a career, a family, and to find the love of my life. I was going to be successful and have the little white house on the hill with the picket fence and perfect family. I found all that. I had all that. So what changed?

It's funny you always hear people say that you want what you cannot have. That the grass is always greener. It is definitely not greener! I had the most perfectly manicured grass (metaphorically and in reality), and yet I wanted something different. I cannot say more; I think it was just different. But if you ask me to tell you what "it" was that I wanted, I could not tell you. I have no idea! How ridiculous is that? How do I explain that to Mark when I don't know what the problem is or what I want? I found myself laughing out loud at myself. I was ridiculous!

I heard a soft knock on my door and then the door opened. Mark stuck his head in and peeked around. "Good morning," he said. "I'm sorry, I heard you laughing, and I thought maybe one of the girls was in here with you. I didn't mean to interrupt your phone call."

I chuckled. "No, I'm not on the phone. I was laughing at myself."

I knew that he was heading to the office this morning, so this was not the time to start this conversation, so I lied. "I realized something that I had done was kind of silly, and I will need to call work to fix it later." Changing the subject, I asked, "So are you heading to the office now?"

"I was just starting to get ready to head in, but I wanted to make sure that you were certain that you did not want me to just take the rest of the week off. It is already Friday, so I can totally take the day off and go back next week." He looked at me as if willing me to say that I wanted him to stay home.

"I should be telling you that you need to go in and take care of things. However, given the circumstances, you could just take the day. I mean, honestly, what difference will one more day make? You were in the accident, too, so the least they could do is cover you for the week after your accident!" I smiled at him, knowing that this was exactly what he wanted to hear.

He smiled a huge smile, flew the door open, and ran and jumped on the bed with me like the kids would do when they were little and we told them that they could sleep with us after they had a nightmare. We both laughed when he slightly overshot the bed and almost landed on his head on the floor. I caught him by his waist and pulled him up to keep him on the bed. Instead of falling off, he ended up falling onto me. We were both laughing about what had happened when Michele and Jordyn appeared in the door.

"Well, we were going to ask if you were alright, but we can see that you are!" Michele said. "Really, guys? The door is wide open!"

Mark and I were still laughing when he quickly replied, "Mom said that I could skip work today, and I got so excited that I launched myself onto the bed."

Then I intervened with "Except he was overzealous and almost missed the bed and landed on his head. I had to grab him to keep him from falling." We both started laughing again at the thought and also at how ridiculous that all probably sounded to the girls.

They both rolled their eyes at each other and headed back down the hall talking to each other about how they would have been in trouble if they were jumping on the beds. I could hear them whispering and giggling as they headed down the stairs.

"Great!" I smacked Mark on the arm. "Now the girls think that we are fooling around. They are giggling!"

"Is that a bad thing?" Mark asked with a smirk on his face. "You remember that song? How did it go? Let's give them something to talk about?" He started singing and reached for me.

I jumped up and swatted at him. "No, stop! I thought we discussed this last night. Or did I dream all that? I don't want to make this a thing for them until or if it does become one! We agreed that we would take things slow, especially when it came to the kids."

"I know. I'm just joking." He looked like a sad puppy who just lost his toy. "But honestly, Laura, you just left a few months ago. It's not like we are just meeting and getting to know each other. We have been together almost our entire adult lives!"

I turned and looked out the window. "I understand that, and I know that it feels weird." I turned back and looked at him. "I also know that it is really confusing to you that I cannot just tell you what happened. Trust me, it is just as confusing to me. I just need you to work with me on this one. Please." I looked at him. "I am just trying to protect the kids."

"I think I understand. But I will be honest, it scares me because it feels like you are giving yourself an escape route. Like doing it this way leaves the door open for you to run again with less guilt this time." He looked down at his hands for a few seconds and then back up at me. "Laura, I don't know if I can handle that again! I barely made it through the first time. I want you back in the worst way, but it will break me if you leave again."

"Mark, I am so sorry. I never meant to hurt you. I know that it was a consequence of my actions, but that was not my intent at all. In fact, it was the reason that I stayed as long as I had. I did not want to hurt you. I just had to do it for myself." I paused. "I cannot say with 100 percent certainty that I will not leave again. I know you want me to promise that I will not, and you are partially correct, I am leaving a door open. But that was the entire reason that I wanted to take it slowly and not just agree to move home like nothing had happened. I need to ease back into this so that as I do it, I can correct whatever the issue was that caused me to leave in the first place. If I do not, we will be right back where we were before when I left the first time. Neither of us wants that. I don't know if I have it in me to do that again, and I do not want to put this family through that again. I need to be sure before I come back. Does that make sense?" I looked at Mark hoping that he would understand.

"I am hearing you, and I do understand what you are saying. I am willing to work with you, but it is going to be difficult for me to trust that you will not hurt me again. I just need to be honest with you. It will take me a lot to fully trust you again." He looked away and stood up. "I love you more than you will ever know. But a part of me wants, no, needs to protect my heart. The heart that I gave to you all those years ago, and you so easily handed it back. So I hope that you understand and respect where I stand."

I looked at him, fighting tears because of the pain that I could see on his face. "I do understand." I did understand what he was saying. It hurt to hear. Even though I knew that I had hurt him, and I was just as afraid of hurting him again as he was of being hurt again. It was painful to hear it from him.

"So where do we go from here?" I asked, not sure if this changed anything that we discussed last night.

He stepped forward and kissed me on the forehead. Then he took my hand and looked me in the eye and said, "Hopefully back to where we started before life went to hell. Only better!" He smiled and walked out the door.

I stood there for a minute just taking in everything that had just happened. I was glad that we had been able to be so open and raw with each other. We needed to be completely open and work through all of it if this was to work between us. I was starting to realize that it was not just me that needed to figure things out. It was us. I was not in this alone. That realization was groundbreaking and yet confusing. If I had tried to fix anything being away and on my own, it is unlikely that we would have ever found our way back to what we had before.

I was still reeling in my head from the events of the past twenty-four hours, not to mention this entire week, when I headed downstairs. I was surprised to see Daniel at the table with the girls. "Oh, good morning, everyone." I walked over and kissed him on the head. "It is a nice surprise to see you here!" I said as I walked over to get my coffee.

Just then, Mark came down the stairs, and I saw the kids exchange a look.

"Okay, you three," I said to them as I took my first sip. "What was that look?" I looked between the three of them.

Daniel looked at Michele who then spoke up and said, "What are you talking about, Mom? You are always so dramatic!" Then she looked at Jordyn and smiled. Then she looked back at Mark and I and said, "Why? What do you think that look was?"

I waited to see if anyone else came forward to say anything before I spoke. "Okay, I don't know what you think you saw, but there was nothing happening with your father and I this morning!"

"Mom, do you have a guilty conscience? We never said anything happened. We never even said that we were giving whatever look you think you saw!" Michele piped up.

"Oh, really?" Mark asked. "Then, Daniel, why are you here instead of in class?"

Daniel looked at Michele and then back at us and chuckled. "I just came by for the show." Michele punched him in the arm. He quickly added, "And to see how Jordyn was doing now that she has been home for a couple of days. I didn't get a chance to come by yesterday to check on her."

"And because your sisters called you with gossip!" I laughed and looked at the three of them again. I then looked at Mark as if to say I told you so. "Alright, we might as well get this out there right now. There is nothing going on like that with your father and I. We are trying to figure this situation out."

Then before I was able to get anything else out, Jordyn chimed in with, "So are you moving home? Is that what you are saying?" She looked at Michele and Daniel with excitement, and they all stared at Mark and me.

I looked at Mark and chose my words carefully, especially in light of the conversation that we had just had in the other room. "I am not, *not* moving back. But we do not want to rush things and make the situation worse. I do still have commitments and responsibilities in New Hampshire, so I will need time to take care of that portion of things. However, while I am here helping Jordyn recover, we will see how things go!" I smiled at them. "That is about all that I can promise for right now. Dad and I have so much to talk about before we would even be close to my moving back permanently. But I love you all very much, and I am very happy that I am here right now. So let's just focus on that for right now, okay?"

They looked at each other and shrugged then agreed that they could live with that for now. The rest of the morning was spent laughing and the kids catching up. Mark headed to the other room to make some calls to the office, and I excused myself to go up to my room to get dressed for the day and call my office. I stood in the window, looking out onto the yard where we had raised our family, practiced soccer, had picnics with family and friends. It all seemed so strange to me. In less than one week, I had gone from being in my first date/outing with another man, even if it was just as friends, to being back in our family home and trying to work things out with the love of my life. I still could not help but to beat myself up about what I had done to the family and to Mark. How would we ever recover from this? Mark's words kept repeating in my brain that it would take a long time for him to trust me again. He did not say it directly, but I betrayed him. I betrayed all of them. I packed up and left their lives. I knew he wanted to be able to, but will he ever really forgive me and be able to move past this?

The phone ringing broke me out of my pity party and jumped me back to reality. When I looked at who was calling, my heart stopped. It was John. Other than thinking about the fact that I had been out last week when the accident happened, I had not given much more thought to our evening out. I walked over and closed my door before I answered. "Hello?"

"Hey, there, stranger!" John started. "I had not heard from you or seen you at the coffee shop all week, and I wanted to make sure that you had not been kidnapped on your way home from our date last weekend." He stopped for me to answer, but I didn't know what to say, so he continued, "Is everything okay? Did I do something?"

"Oh no! It was nothing you did!" I apologized, now feeling bad for not thinking about it before. "I am so sorry! When I got home after our outing, I turned my phone on to find out that my husband and girls had been in an accident. I had to run back to Connecticut to be with them. I should have let you know that I was not around."

"Oh no, I'm so sorry. Is everyone alright?" John sounded sincere if not a bit hesitant.

"Yes, well at least better now. My middle daughter was hurt pretty badly and was in the hospital for a few days and had to have two surgeries. My youngest had several stitches but is alright. My husband was fine with just some bumps and bruises and emotional damage. It looks like everyone should make a full recovery. The car on the other hand was a total loss."

"Well, the car can be replaced, but they cannot be. I am happy to hear that the girls are going to be alright. And that your…husband…was unharmed." I could hear the change in his voice when he said husband. "I'm sorry. I did not mean to intrude on your time. I was just concerned and wanted to make sure that everything was alright and that you were not avoiding me for some reason." Then he paused a bit and added, "But I can certainly see why you might. I wish you the best, Laura. I hope to see you around the coffee shop again some time. Goodbye." He had hung up before I could say anything else.

I stared at the phone for a minute thinking how odd that call was and feeling bad that I had not thought to text him to tell him what had happened. Honestly, I had not given him much thought. For me, it was a nice evening out, and it felt good to do something other than just go home to an empty apartment. I enjoyed his company, and it was nice to have a man's attention again, but that was the extent of it for me. I felt bad that he may have thought more of it. I also would have sworn that we had discussed the fact that I was still married, so his reaction took me aback a bit.

With the circumstances of the last twenty-four hours, this complication was not something that I wanted to entertain. He was someone that I met casually that I just happened to bump into almost daily getting my morning coffee. We decided to eat dinner at the same time, in the same place one evening, and that was it. If that was it, why was it bothering me? Maybe I'm just being ridiculous. I was feeling bad because I had hurt someone else's feelings, and after my discussion with Mark earlier, I was hypersensitive to it. That was what it was. I am not going to give it another thought for right now. I have things that I needed to work through, and that was the most important thing. Alright, that was settled.

I went about getting ready for the day and called my office. I wanted to talk to them about taking more time off to stay with Jordyn until at least her first follow-up appointments with her doctors so that we could make sure that she was healing well and that she did not have any more residual effects that we had been seeing with her blood pressure. It was a difficult call as they were not thrilled that

I was going to be out at least another week. Thankfully, the push in my department was less at the beginning of the school year than it was at the end. Although this was when they start molding how the year will go for preparation for graduate schools, so it was still busy. Plus, with my just having started within the past few months, this was not a good look for me.

As much as I did not want to lose my job, for several reasons, I could not help but to think how it would make my decision, and return, that much easier. Then I would only have the apartment and breaking my lease and then moving all my stuff back home to think about. Unfortunately, that was not the only thing that I had to consider.

I finished up and went to check on Jordyn. She was progressing extremely well with getting around and being somewhat independent although she was still tiring easily and taking a lot of naps. I checked in on her and found that she was sitting on her bed fighting with her sling.

"Can I help?" I asked as I walked toward her.

"I am literally counting the days until this stupid thing comes off and I don't feel like Grandma anymore! It is so frustrating being this crippled!" She was near tears.

"Sweetheart, this is not crippled. If you would like, I can take you on a field trip to the children's hospital and you can see what it is really like to be disabled as a child!" I smiled at her. "Do you remember when I took you to the homeless shelter when you were all acting like spoiled brats around Christmas? Every one of you had the most expensive things on your Santa lists, and I was gently trying to remind you that every Christmas movie that we watched had homemade toys, so not to expect too much from Santa."

"Oh, I remember!" Jordyn laughed. "I thought Michele was going to lose her mind when her friend told her what she was expecting to get from Santa, and we were visiting kids in a shelter that had nothing." Then she paused and looked serious. "But it was the single best Christmas. That was the year that we started buying gifts for all the kids in the shelter. It was an amazing feeling."

"It was honestly one of my favorite parts of Christmas too. Getting the list from Sister Peter in November and taking you kids shopping for each child. One toy and one necessity. Then setting up the dining room like Santa's workshop and wrapping and tagging each of them. It was an amazing feeling." I was smiling at the thought of it again. "But the even better feeling was loading up the van with the bags of toys and dropping them at the shelter on Christmas Eve so that the nuns could put them under the tree for the kids in the morning."

"Yeah, that was pretty cool. You told us that we were just helping Santa to deliver some extra presents because their mommies and daddies needed help." Jordyn smiled at me. "At least until we stopped believing. I always wanted to stay to see the kids' faces."

I smiled. "Sister Peter asked me to stay one time. She said, 'Don't you want to see them so they can thank you?' I told her no. I want them to have the same magic of Christmas that every other kid has Christmas morning. They have little else, let's not take that too!" I smiled at the thought. "I really miss doing that." I sighed and looked down at my hands then mumbled under my breath, "Just another thing that we became too busy for."

"What?" Jordyn asked me.

"Oh, sorry. I was just saying I was mad at myself for not making the time to continue that. Life just got so busy that I seemed to have let go of the important things that I wish I had not."

Jordyn looked at me and smiled. "Are you starting to rethink your…ummm…life decisions?"

I thought about how I was going to respond. "I have always second-guessed how I did anything. Did I do it right? Could I have done things differently? So in a way, yes. And like I told you all this morning, we are working towards a resolution. Am I sorry I did it? Maybe to some degree. But it was necessary to get me out of the position that I was feeling that I was in. Sometimes you just have to shake things up to see where you will land. Hopefully, it is in a better place than I was." She gave me a kind of shocked look. "I mean mentally. Not physically. I am no good to anyone else if I cannot get my head straightened out! Right here is where I want to be!" I hugged her as tight as I could without hurting her.

I headed downstairs to try to go through my emails while she lay down to rest. Her blood pressure was still up and down, which could be part of why she was so tired, in addition to just recovering from her ordeal. This was still of concern to me, but it was definitely going in the right direction. Just another reason that I need to stay and talk to her doctors.

Mark had taken the day off but had several errands to run and headed out late morning saying that he would be back in a few hours. I spent the time bouncing between reading my emails, getting onto my work email, and trying to take care of some things from a distance and watching movies. I made lunch for Jordyn and I and threw in a load of laundry, including everyone's bloody clothes from the accident. It was emotional all the way around. First, being in our home doing all the normal things that I had always done but with more time to do those things than was normal for me. Also, cleaning up from the accident and reliving the thought that I could have lost all of it in the blink of an eye.

It was one thing for me to leave all of it, with the knowledge that I could come back and everything would be here just as it was when I closed that door. But the realization that the accident could have changed everything in my life was almost too much. I found myself standing in the laundry room crying about what could have happened and that I would have regretted so much. You always hear how you need to tell people that you love them because they can be gone in a moment. It's overwhelming when that hits so close to home.

I regained my composure and headed back up to the kitchen. When I walked into the kitchen, Mark was standing by the table looking down at my phone. He had stopped and picked up sushi for us.

I smiled and said, "How was your afternoon? Did you get everything done that you needed to?" I took the food into the kitchen and started plating it for everyone. Mark did not answer right away, so I turned to look at him.

"Hello? Did you hear me?" Mark just stood there with a blank stare on his face. "Mark?" I asked, now starting to get a little concerned.

"Yeah…sorry. It was fine." He looked up at me as if he wanted to say something but was pausing like he did not know how to form the words.

"Mark," I said as I stepped toward him. "Are you alright? Did something happen? You are starting to scare me!" My voice cracked a little with the last part. I was fighting panic. I was not sure that I could handle anything else happening right now.

"I'm fine. Nothing has happened…I don't think. At least I hope not," he answered, still looking dazed.

"Mark, seriously, open your mouth and speak, please! You are freaking me out!" I stood staring at him with my hands on my hips, getting annoyed.

He stared at me for a minute before saying, "Who is John?"

I stood staring at him, a little confused and not quite understanding what he was asking at first. Then I remembered he was staring at my phone when I walked into the kitchen. I looked down at my phone and saw a notification of a text message. I looked back at him.

"Are you talking about something on there?" I pointed to my phone. "Did I get a message from someone? Or were you looking in my phone?" I more accused than asked.

"Your phone was making noises when I came in, and I saw his name come up with a heart. I did not go through your phone. Why are you worried? Do you have something to hide? Or is it even any of my business? Damn, Laura. I didn't expect that there was ever going to be someone else. Is there someone else?" He was spiraling, and I was not in the mood to fight at all about this. It was a ridiculous argument, and I did not have the energy to have it right now.

I waited until he was finished spitting out the questions, and then I said, "Are you done now?" While I stood and waited for him to respond, I opened my phone to the messages so that I could see what he had seen. There was a message from John saying that he apologized for being so short with me the last time that we spoke and that he was sorry to hear about my family. He then said he hopes everyone was doing well and that he sent his best wishes and ended it with a heart. That must have been what Mark had seen.

"First of all, there is no one else. John is a gentleman that I met at the coffee shop that I go to every morning, and I see him daily. He was sending his well wishes for everyone's recovery and ended his message with a heart. There is nothing for you to be concerned about."

Mark looked relieved but still guarded. I knew that this all went back to his trust issues with me, but another man was not something that was our problem and would never be an issue for us.

I looked at Mark and took a step toward him. "I would hope that you would know me well enough by now to know that I," I paused for dramatic effect, "could not handle more than one man because *you* are more than enough to handle already!" I laughed, hoping to break the ice from this tense moment. He looked away, and I did see him crack a smile. Then I turned his head back toward me. "I joke, but I am serious. You have no reason to worry about anyone else. It has always been you. The problem is not even you, it is us, our circumstances, my handling of those circumstances, but never you or any desire or interest in anyone else. I hope with all of my heart that even if you are not sure about trusting me with your heart right now that you can trust me on!"

He looked at me and smiled. "I do. I'm sorry that I reacted like that. I just feel really." He paused and looked away as if he was embarrassed. "I feel ridiculously vulnerable right now when it comes to you. It is not a feeling that I like at all!"

I looked at him, seeing the man that I fell in love with and still loved so deeply. "I am so sorry that I have hurt you like I have. I will do everything in my power to try to fix it." *Without losing myself,* I thought.

Mark smiled at me and looked as if he were about to lean in for a kiss when we heard Jordyn coming down the stairs.

"Do I smell sushi rolls and dumplings?"

We both took a step back as if we were doing something wrong and turned toward Jordyn. She stopped immediately when she saw us. "Did I interrupt something? You two look like we used to when you were catching us doing something wrong!"

"No!" I said maybe just a little too quickly. "I was just asking Dad how his afternoon was and was telling him about what I was able to get accomplished today. I watched a whole movie and put laundry in. Oh, and I made us lunch! Woohoo, I am feeling so accomplished." I joked, trying to be as normal as I possibly could be after what just happened.

"Where is Michele?" Mark asked. "I think she was planning to be home in time for dinner. Her class should have been out almost two hours ago. Has anyone heard from her?"

Jordyn and I looked at each other and shook our heads no. I said, "Well, I haven't really had my phone on me." I glanced at it to see if she messaged me. "No, I don't have anything."

When I looked up, Mark was looking at me with a strange look on his face. We had to table our discussion, but it was clearly not over yet. Unfortunately, it would have to wait.

Mark called Michele, who came in as we were almost finished with dinner. While she caught up on the day's events with Mark and Jordyn, I ran to swap the laundry. I paused for a minute to process what had happened but more so of Mark's reaction to the messages. I had not given much thought to his being upset about someone sending me messages. It was odd being in this situation. When we dated years ago, there were no cell phones or social media. There was not instant access to anyone, so we never thought about anything like this. I had given John my information so that we could chat as we needed to and to get the information for our night out. A night that I was starting to regret, not because it was romantic or anything, but because I was afraid how Mark would feel about it if he were to find out.

That put me in another dilemma. *Do I tell him and risk hurting him more or losing him? Or do I continue to lie to him and keep it from him to protect him and us?* I could justify it in that it was not a date. It was two people who knew one another going out to grab dinner and have a fun conversation. It was not romantic, and it was just nice to get out of the house and have a conversation with someone other than the doorman or my coffee barista. It was nothing more than the equivalent of going out with my friends. But I do not think that Mark will see it that way.

Footsteps on the stairs brought me out of my thoughts when I realized that I had been downstairs for quite a while longer than I would normally have been. It was Mark coming to check on me. I busied myself with pulling laundry out of the dryer and folding it.

"Laura, are you alright? I could have done three loads in the time that you've been down here." He stopped to see my reaction, but I continued to fold. "Are you avoiding us, or is something going on?"

"Why would I be avoiding anyone, Mark?" I looked at him while still folding. My mind was racing trying to figure out how to get out of this conversation that was already making me uncomfortable. "I just needed a minute. This is all still so overwhelming to me. The house, the kids, you, this entire situation after the accident. I am trying to figure things out that will work for everyone after being thrown into this unexpectedly. Not to mention the fact that our daughter is recovering from two major surgeries and there is still something going on with her blood pressure. So it's a lot right now."

"I know." He said looking down. "Then I go and add stress by freaking out unnecessarily about that message. I'm sure that did not help. I'm sorry. I'm just so damned insecure about you since you left. I never in a million years would have expected you to just up and walk out, so now I overthink everything as if I don't really know you. I hope you understand."

What is happening right now? Here I am trying to decide whether I should tell him about something that was very innocent, and I was feeling guilty about it, and he is apologizing for feeling the way that I was responsible for making him feel. This was starting to feel like an episode of the *Twilight Zone*! Well, that just clinched my decision. I clearly could not tell him because that would just crush him.

"Mark, you have nothing to apologize for! You did nothing wrong. I would have reacted the same way if I was in your shoes."

"I believe you did once," Mark said. Then he looked up and smiled at me. "Do you remember the time that I had gone out to inspect that job in Chaplin and you decided you would surprise me because you were home that day and close by? Then when you got there, I was talking to the female contractor. Your reaction was so over the top. I had never seen you like that before!"

"Well, I'm sorry, but there is no way that you would have been acting like that with any male contractor! She was being totally inappropriate, and you were either completely oblivious to it or you were sucking up every moment of it. I was just glad that I intervened when I did because she was going in for the kill shot!"

"Laura, she was not going in for anything."

"You are so blind! She was posed and ready to lean into you. She nearly toppled over when I called out to you because she was leaning so close to you." I was getting irritated all over again just thinking about walking in and seeing that woman trying to make the moves on my husband and at work no less! The one place you would think would be a safe place. Even more annoying was that he was not stopping her.

"She was leaning over looking at the blueprints and you startled her by yelling. Of course, she almost fell over!"

"Oh, really? Then when you got home, she was texting you with cute little smiley faces. What was that all about?" I looked to see his reaction, which was one of surprise. It felt like someone kicked me in the stomach.

"You saw those?" He looked surprised and sad. He looked down at his hands. "I'm sorry, Laura. Why didn't you tell me you saw them?"

Sorry, what did he mean sorry? Now I wish I had not even told him about those. All these years it had bothered me, but nothing more came of it, so I had forgotten about it. Although my ears did perk up if he ever mentioned a woman on any of the jobs. I did not think that I wanted to know any more, but part of me was pushing to know.

"What do you mean you are sorry? Sorry that I saw them or sorry about something more?"

He quickly looked up at me and looked hurt. "Laura, I would never do anything inappropriate. I love you, and I would never risk losing you for anything or anyone else. I am sorry that you saw those. If you had looked further, you would have seen that I asked her to kindly forward all communication through the company email from that point forward. I also reminded her whenever I saw her that I was married. It became so much of an issue that I had someone else finish that job."

"You never told me that! I thought you had finished it or been pulled off of that one to do another one." I blushed a little. I should have known better than to even think anything like that. I had never known anyone more loyal than he had been from the day we met. Loyal to me, his friends, even his worthless college roommate who spent more time hitting on me and trying to steal me away from Mark than he did going to class. Every time I would tell Mark about it, he would just laugh and say, "Yeah, that's Dave! He thinks he's a lady's man, but he really isn't. He's harmless."

Mark stepped forward and took my hand. "I wish you had told me how you felt about all of this all those years ago. I don't ever want there to be anything that we cannot talk through or that you cannot tell me how you feel so that we can fix the situation. I would have handed that job off long before I did if I had known that you were that upset about it." Then he looked down and paused for a couple of seconds. Then he looked at me and said, "I feel even worse that I did not see how it made you feel. That is unforgivable."

I reached forward and touched his face. "Mark, there is nothing to forgive. I was jealous, an emotion that does not happen often, and I thought I was being ridiculous. I trusted you, and we got through it. But I do promise that I will be more open about my feelings and talk to you about things that are bothering me. I promise." I was already breaking my promise because it was bothering me that I had not told him about going out to dinner with John. However, there was nothing to tell. I was not going to cause undue pain to him. There was nothing more to the story, so we were going to bury that one.

I hugged Mark and told him I would be up in just a couple of minutes when the laundry was all set. He headed upstairs to pick up from dinner and take a shower.

We had a quiet evening, and everyone decided to go to bed early. Tomorrow was Saturday, the one-week anniversary of the accident. Since Jordyn was feeling better every day, although a bit tired, we decided to get her out of the house and take a drive. It would do her some good to get out of the house. We just could not have her do anything strenuous. We all decided on a plan to take a drive to the shoreline and grab lunch and ice cream. We would have her back in a few hours just in time for her afternoon nap. I was hoping that getting her out of the house and forcing her to stay up a little longer would start her on the track to feeling more normal. I was still concerned that she was sleeping so much after so many days, along with her roller coaster blood-pressure readings. We would definitely be discussing that more with the doctor on our first follow-up visit.

After getting Jordyn tucked in and settled, I headed to my room. I passed Mark's room and noticed the door was open. Mark was sitting on the bed staring at his feet. I stopped to say good night. He didn't notice that I was standing there. I walked up to the door and knocked lightly. "Hey, I was just stopping to say good night. Are you alright?"

He didn't answer right away or look up, so I took another step forward. He looked up at me, and I could tell he had either been crying or was getting ready to.

"Do you think we can fix this?" he asked. He turned his head away from me. "You keep saying that you are trying to figure things out. I don't even know what things you need to figure out. I still have no idea what it was that happened or that I did to make you leave." His voice started to crack, so he stopped.

I did not even know how to answer him. At this moment, I could not remember what it was that caused me to pack up and just walk out the door. I knew that I was feeling like I was drowning and that I could not breathe.

"Mark, there was not something that happened or anything that you did. It was me. I know that this sounds absurd, but I cannot tell you with 100 percent certainty that I know what made me leave."

He looked at me as if I had just told him that I had been abducted by aliens. He looked completely baffled and confused. "What do you mean you do not know what made you leave? You uprooted your entire life, our entire life, and walked out, and you cannot tell me why? Who does that?" His confusion was turning to slight anger.

"I can tell you that I was feeling completely overwhelmed and like I was drowning. I truly felt that if I did not get out as soon as possible, I was going to break. I think it was just everything. It was the amount of responsibility that I had between work, the kids' activities, the household chores, worrying about the kids' school and college prep, just all of it. I had been doing it for so long that I was just worn down." He started to say something, and I held my hand up. "I know what you are about to say. The kids were almost done and things would get easier. Believe me, when I am sitting alone in my apartment with nothing and no one, I tell myself that and ask why I didn't wait." I paused and stared at the ceiling for a minute. "Mark, no one is more confused or upset about the choices I made than I am. If I could turn back time and relive it, I would fix all of this. But I felt that I had no choice at the time. So I did what I had to do. Now I have to live with the consequences."

Mark looked at me for a long time. I could see that he was trying to make sense of it all. "I guess I just don't understand why you never told me any of this. Did you not trust me enough to tell me? Or did you not think that I would understand? Trust me, I totally understand that feeling. Sometimes it was overwhelming, but I never, in a million years, would have ever thought that the only answer was to walk out the door and leave you or the kids. You are my entire world. So I guess you will have to forgive me if I just cannot wrap my head around that part of all of this."

I was a little taken aback by his words. I was not asking him to forgive me. I had just asked that he try to understand what I was saying. He was not wrong. If you were to poll any other household, the majority would say that they feel the way that I did almost daily. But there are few, if any, of those people who just run away from everything and everyone as a fix.

"You asked a question, Mark, and I was trying to answer it the best that I could. I understand that you are angry with me. You have every right to be. I did not look at it as if I was abandoning you or the kids. I looked at it as I was saving myself. You are not wrong, I did abandon you all. There is no way around that. I am the one that should be asking for forgiveness. I am grateful for the fact that any of you are even speaking to me, much less that you let me back into your lives and that you want to try to make things work. But please understand that it is not like I just fell out of bed and I am climbing back in. I jumped for a reason. So in order for this to work, I need to resolve the problem."

There was a long silence. Finally, Mark looked at me and said, "Well, I guess you will need to figure that part out. I will just be waiting right here while you do that."

I stared incredulously at him. I had not seen this side of Mark in quite some time. He was being snarky and deliberately argumentative. It hurt me to know that I had been the cause of this behavior because it was very out of character for him. He was that guy that everyone loved. He was funny and witty, and people just tend to gravitate toward him. This was not an attractive side of him. During any other argument, pre-abandonment, I would have used that leverage and pointed it out to him. However, given the circumstances, I felt that I was deserving of his anger.

"Mark, I understand that you are hurting and you will be up and down with that. I deserve it, and I will take it this time." I turned to walk out of the room. I stopped and turned back to look at him. He looked as if he was about to try to stop me. "For what it is worth," I said. "I am sorry. For everything! Good night, Mark." Then I turned and left before either of us could say anything more.

I went into my room, closed the door, and took a breath for the first time in the last several minutes. I had not realized that I was holding my breath until that moment. As much as the last several conversations with Mark where difficult to have, I was feeling good about where we were. Both of us had things that were bothering us and that we needed to get off our chests. We were making progress with that. I had known that coming back was not going to be Mark standing at the front door as if waiting for me to come home from work. I had done a lot of damage by leaving. I needed to repair that damage.

I just hoped that I was able to repair enough of it that would allow us to be back to as normal as possible. I was terrified that we would do all this work to try to fix things just to find out that we could not fix it. Where would that leave this family? I had already put the kids through so much. Was I really willing to take the chance of making things worse? The bigger question was whether I was willing to just continue to walk away without trying to fix things.

Sometimes, you need to walk away from a situation in order to see exactly what you need to see. I can see now that the things that I was allowing to wear me down were all temporary. Had I just waited a little longer, it all would have resolved itself. What scared me was that I knew that the day-to-day stresses would be relieved very soon, and yet I still left. So there had to be more to all of it than I was either realizing or I was not acknowledging.

As much as I was not a fan, and even with as independent as I was, if I cannot figure out what really caused me to leave, I was going to need to do something extreme and possibly start to see a professional to try to get answers. Anyone who knew me knew that I was opposed to counseling. I had never felt that I would be able to open up enough for it to work. Counseling is fine for some people, and some need it. But the thought of opening up my life, my soul, to a complete stranger made me want to run farther than I did the last time. I was just not sure that it was something that I could do. However, given the alternative of losing everything that I love forever, I will do whatever it takes to make the repairs and get my family and my life back. I was just hoping that it will not come down to that.

It took a while for me to fall asleep once I had made the decision to seek professional help if necessary, but I was able to eventually sleep. It was not a good sleep though. I tossed and turned and had terrible dreams that were so realistic that I was confused when I awoke and I was in the guest room. Each time I fell back to sleep, the dreams were worse than the one before. I was starting to think that the universe was either trying to tell me something or it was punishing me. Either way, sleep was not my friend. Sometime around 3:00 a.m., I opened my phone and started scrolling social media because I was afraid to go back to sleep and have another dream.

I must have dozed off sometime around sunrise. I was not sure because I was scrolling aimlessly and jumped down a rabbit hole of mindless videos. When I awoke, the sun was high enough in the sky that it was coming in my window. That had to mean it was close to 9:00 a.m. I struggled to clear the fog from my head and got myself up and ready for my day.

When I opened my door, there was a note from Mark. It simply read "I'm sorry."

I checked on Jordyn and made sure she was set for the day with her medications, food, and was able to get dressed. I did what I had always done best and smiled through it all so that no one knew anything was wrong. I grabbed a cup of coffee and finished up the laundry that I had started the night before. I sat down at the table to finish my coffee and check my email messages. There was an email from my manager advising that she needed to speak with me as soon as possible about some urgent business. I called her right away.

"Hi, Laura. Thank you for getting back to me so quickly. I know that you are in the middle of a family crisis, but we have some things that have come up here, and we are going to need you back in the office as soon as possible. When do you think you will be able to get back?"

I was stunned. "I thought that Brian was handling things while I was out. Is it something that he cannot cover?" I asked. My mind was racing. I did not want to lose my job, but I also did not feel that I was ready to leave Jordyn on her own quite yet. She was still struggling to do simple things like dressing.

"Well, he is to an extent. However, there are things that he cannot handle. Things for which you were specifically hired to handle. That was why we hired someone with a law degree and background." She paused for a minute. "Laura, I would never ask you to come back with your family circumstances being what they are. But this has come down from the Board. I tried to explain the severity of your situation. Unfortunately, this is something that they are not able to put off."

She sounded sincerely sorry, so it was hard to be upset with her. More concerning was the fact that the Board was involved, which also meant that my position was in the spotlight and under scrutiny. I really did not need this pressure right now. Not with everything else that was happening right now.

I was still trying to figure out what I was going to do when she asked, "How is your daughter and family? I cannot imagine how that must have felt being so far away when you got the news." That comment hit hard. It was difficult, but to have someone else point that out just hurt.

"They are doing well under the circumstances. My youngest had stitches but is doing fine. My husband had some bumps and bruises, not to mention the emotional scars, but is doing alright. My middle daughter took the brunt of the crash. She was in the direct line of fire and had to have two major surgeries to repair her injuries. She is doing as well as can be expected being less than a week from the accident. She still has some medical concerns that we are watching closely, which is why I am still here. Plus, she is still not able to do most daily activities like dressing or preparing food. She is still sleeping a good majority of the time just trying to heal." I was rambling, and I knew it, but I needed her to understand that I could not just leave at this moment.

"Laura, I am so sorry, and I completely understand that you do not want to leave her. If I were in your position, I would feel exactly the same way." She paused for a moment as if trying to gauge what to say next. "What do you want me to tell the Board?"

I thought about it for a moment and asked, "How soon do they need to have me back there?" I was thinking about the appointment that Jordyn had coming up that I really wanted to go to with her since her blood pressure was still an issue. "Maybe we can figure something out that I might be able to work a shortened week so that I could have longer weekends to be able to split my time. Is it something that I could handle from a distance for the time being?" I was grasping at straws, but I needed to be able to work this out. I was feeling like I was being backed into a corner.

"I honestly do not know. How about we do this, I will go and talk to the Board a bit more about the situation and your suggestions. Once I have some more detail from them, I will let you know what they say. If they ask, what was your plan for a return if we had not had this discussion? I would like to have something as a jumping-off point."

I froze. I had not really had a plan. For what feels like the first time in my life, I was just winging it. I knew that this was where I wanted to be, needed to be, and I was just doing it. I had not thought it out and had a plan for a return.

"I am really not sure," I said. "I have been playing it by ear as far as waiting to see how her treatment and recovery goes. She was just released from the hospital a couple of days ago, and she is still settling in. I guess I am still reeling from the entire ordeal, so I'm not thinking very far ahead."

"As is to be expected," she said very supportively. "You know that men see these family situations differently than women usually do. I completely understand your position and desire to be home with your family. However, they will see it as a business need. We will just need to try to find some common ground that everyone can agree on. I would hate to lose you over a situation like this especially since you just got here and are still settling in. I will let you know what they suggest when they get back to me, and we can talk then. In the meantime, I hope things continue to improve for your family. Give my best to everyone, and if you need anything, please let me know. Goodbye, Laura."

I was barely able to get a "Goodbye" out before she disconnected the call. I was not sure how I was feeling at the moment. I did not want to lose my job. I had never been fired from any job I ever had, not even the terrible high school jobs everyone gets for spending money. I always prided myself on doing the best I could in any situation. "If you are going to do something, do it well," my grandmother always told me. I did not want to ruin my track record now.

On the other hand, I did not want to be forced to leave my daughter, my family before I felt that I was ready to or that they were ready. My family comes before anything else. There was nothing that was going to stand in the way of that.

I was still feeling annoyed when Mark came into the house. He must have been out at the gym the way he was dressed and all sweaty.

"Well, well, you finally decided to get up?" he joked. "Rough night or avoiding me?" He laughed and grabbed a cup of coffee.

"I just didn't sleep well," I said distractedly.

Mark looked at me with concern. "Is everything alright? You seem distracted. Or still angry with me?" He sipped his coffee and watched me over the cup rim.

"Oh, no, sorry. Just work stuff. I just got off the phone with the office."

"Is everything alright?" Then as if slightly panicked, he asked, "Do you need to get back?" Then he looked at me as if he didn't really want the answer.

"No, nothing urgent. It's fine." Then as if to change the subject, I asked, "So are we going for a drive? I thought that was the plan." Then I jokingly said, "If so, you need to go shower because I'm not sitting in a car that long with you smelling like that!" Then I laughed and made faces as if something smelled terrible.

Mark took that and ran with it, lunging toward me as if to make me smell his armpits. I laughed and fought him off, feigning that I was fainting. We both laughed just like we used to do all the time. I had definitely missed that. I missed him and our friendship. I missed how close we had been.

As if he could read my mind, he looked at me and said, "Yeah, I miss it too." Then he kissed my forehead, smiled at me, and turned to head upstairs. "I'm going to take a shower. Do you want to gather the troops?"

"On it!" I said, still wrapped up in the moment we just shared. It was all these little things that were making me question everything that I had done. And now everything that I was doing.

I got the girls, and we put together everything that we might need for the trip, including extra pillows and a couple of blankets to make sure Jordyn was comfortable sitting that long. I grabbed her medications, snacks, and drinks for the ride. Of course, we would be stopping for coffee, and eventually lunch, but in the meantime, we would have everything that we needed. We were all set up and the car was all packed when Mark came down from his shower.

"Are we ready to go?" he asked.

"We are all packed and ready. I think we have everything that we need," I said as if I was reporting to a superior officer.

The girls were walking out the door, and Mark paused to look at me. "I have everything I need right here." Then he smiled at me and headed out to the car.

It took me a few seconds to follow him. I was fighting back tears and did not want him or the girls to see me like that. I pretended that I had to grab something. I had the man and a love that most people spend their entire lives looking for and never find it. His love for me was so open and amazing that you just needed to look at him with me to see it. Our friends and family always joked, saying "Get a room" when we had gatherings. So who in their right mind would throw that away?

I ran out and hopped in the car and said "Alright, let's go!" and off we went.

We drove through town and out along the back roads down to the shore. The weather was perfect. It was a crisp fall day. The leaves were turning, so it was colorful, and the humidity had left, so the colors were clear and bright. As we drove along the shore, we saw all the little shops still holding out for business that had died down significantly since the summer days. The shoreline was always busy and festive during the summer months, but as fall sets in, it became more and more deserted. While still beautiful, the cooler weather brought fewer people. By late fall, it was like a ghost town. As much as I loved the shore, we would never venture this way off season as it seemed so sad and lonely.

"Well, we got here just in time!" Mark said. "Another week and it would be deserted. Mom doesn't come here when it's deserted."

It was starting to feel like Mark was inside my head. Whatever I was thinking, he said. I shook it off and said, "Well, it is too sad and lonely. Then I cannot enjoy it." Then I looked at him and said, "Now, if we drove the shoreline down south, then I could anytime."

Mark rolled his eyes at me, and we all laughed.

It was a long-standing joke that I had wanted to move south for years, but Mark was adamant that he would not move. He did not like the heat and did not see the attraction to the south. He liked to visit there but had no interest in moving. I was always talking about moving south, and he would always jokingly argue against it. It was ironic that when I did move away, I had gone north and not south.

We continued the length of the shoreline into Rhode Island and stopped for lunch at a little out-of-the-way place that was right on the water. We enjoyed a delicious seafood lunch and a short stroll on the main street in town. I would have loved to have done a little shopping, but I was watching Jordyn who was wearing out quickly.

"Maybe we should think about getting back so Jordyn can get some rest." I smiled at her. "We have been out for a few hours now. This is the longest that you have stayed up in days. Plus, your pain medication is going to kick in again soon, and you are going to get sleepy."

We headed back to the car and settled in for the ride back. Everyone was quiet on the ride home. We had full bellies, and the day was warming up, so we were all feeling a little sleepy. I was lost in thought, and when I looked over at Mark, it looked like he was too.

I checked the back seat and saw both girls starting to doze off. I leaned toward Mark and whispered, "Penny for your thoughts."

He did not answer right away. He glanced over at me and into the back seat. "They are worth a lot more than that!" he joked. I chuckled. Then he continued, "I was just thinking that I miss this. I don't want today to end."

We were both quiet for several minutes. "Laura," he continued. "Do you ever miss this? Miss us?"

I smiled and leaned toward him so that he could see my face better. "I miss all of it!"

He smiled, and we drove the rest of the way home in silence.

I was coming to the realization that even if the Board came back willing to work with me on either being able to work short weeks or remotely, I was not sure that I wanted to stay in that position. If I stay there, it will mean that I would have to go back to the apartment. Going back to the apartment would mean leaving again. I did not want to leave again. I was truly not sure that I ever wanted to leave. I do know that something needed to change, and the change that

I forced caused a domino effect that shook our life and put it into balance.

It certainly was not without negative effects, such as hurting those that I love more than life itself and causing Mark to now distrust me. I would need to spend the rest of my days trying to make up for the pain that I caused them and showing Mark that he can trust me again. It would be a long process, but we had a solid foundation, so I was confident that we could do this. Now I just needed to discuss this with Mark. That would mean that we would need to be alone.

When we got home, we unpacked the car. I brought Jordyn inside and got her settled into her room. She was exhausted from the day and was struggling. I checked her blood pressure, and it was on the lower side but better than it had been. I was hoping that the salt from the seafood would also help to raise it a little but in a healthy way.

I headed back downstairs to help to unpack and put everything away. Mark was standing in the kitchen staring off into space. I hesitated to go into the kitchen because I did not want to intrude on his thoughts. After a couple of minutes, he started to wander aimlessly around the kitchen. I figured it was safe to come in, so I acted like I had just come down the stairs and walked in.

"Is she all set?" he asked.

"Yes, she was really tired. I checked her blood pressure, and it is still on the low side but a bit better. I was hoping that it would have improved by now to match what they thought was causing it. It is starting to worry me that we are not seeing much improvement so long after the accident and surgeries. I'm thinking that we might want to talk to her primary care about getting a specialist just to be sure that we cover all bases." I looked at him as if for his agreement.

He was staring at me but did not seem to have heard a word that I said. I stared back at him, slightly annoyed. "Hello? Mark, did you hear anything that I said?"

He shook his head as if he was clearing it. "Huh? Yeah, sorry, I heard you." Then he just continued to look at me. "Laura, I don't know how I am going to handle any of this without you. Or how I am going to be able to let you go again. The thought that at some point you are going to get in your car and leave again crushes me. I feel like I cannot breathe when I think about it." He looked away.

I walked over to him and turned his face to look at me. "Hey," I said. "Stop thinking about it."

"How can I stop? I have begged the universe every night to bring you home. I feel like the accident was my fault. I asked so much that I had to sacrifice something to have you come home. But the universe has a cruel way of doing things. You came home but only for a little while. It is going to tear me apart to lose you again. I don't think I can bear it."

"What if I were to say that you would not have to?" I asked. I stared deep into his eyes. "Mark, I was a fool. I was selfish and stupid. I never should have left. I was completely overwhelmed, and I did not know what else to do other than remove myself from it. I felt as if I was suffocating and could not catch my breath. I should have talked to you, but I felt like you were part of the problem. Being away from you, from the kids has been the hardest thing I have ever done. Yeah, in the beginning, the independence and the newness of the situation was exciting. Then the loneliness set in. The lack of purpose. I am a mom, a wife well before I am anything else. I pushed both of those things away, and then I lost myself. I thought I was 'finding' myself by leaving, but I realized that I had found my true self, right here, with you."

Mark was looking at me with excitement and hesitation. I smiled at him and said, "So I was thinking. Since I have a one-year lease and don't want to lose the money, what would you think about having a getaway place? Just you and I, on the weekends or days we just need to get away." I looked at him. "I don't want to jump back into anything. Maybe we could date again, get to know each other." Then I smiled and giggled. "And just for the record, there will be no hanky-panky on the first date!" I threw my head back and laughed.

Mark grabbed me in a huge hug. Then he nestled his face in my ear. "We will see about that." He laughed.

After a couple of minutes, he pulled back and looked me in the eye. "Are you absolutely certain about this? I was serious when I said that I cannot go through this again. The thought of losing you again is overwhelming and makes me feel like I'm having a heart attack." He started to tear up. "Laura, I have been so empty since you left. You are my entire world, and my world crashed."

I grabbed his face in both of my hands and said very softly, "I am one thousand percent certain that there is nowhere in the world that I want to be other than right here with you. Nowhere!"

Then I kissed him. It was just like when we first met. So much passion and feeling. When we were finished kissing, I stepped back.

"Now *that* is what we have been missing!" I smiled.

Mark smiled at me. "What are we going to tell the kids? And what are you going to do about your job?"

I thought about it for a second. "I would really like to just wait a little while to tell the kids." Mark looked as if he was deflating. "*Only* because I would like to share this just between us for a little while. I want to enjoy every minute of it with just you for now."

He smiled and looked relieved.

"As to my job." I paused, thinking about my conversation from earlier. "I think that may be resolving itself as we speak. The Board wanted me to cut my trip short because they think that what they need from me is more important than what my family needs. I am certain that there is some legal precedent that they are violating, but more importantly, what would make them think that that job, or that they would ever be more important than my family, is beyond me."

"Ohhhh," Mark said. "That is not good! They clearly do not know you!" He stepped forward and wrapped his arms around me. "Well, it is their loss because you are amazing at anything that you do. Besides, I would rather have you here because we appreciate you much more than they do!"

The emotions flowing through me at this moment were incredible and confusing. The feeling of relief that I had was immense. I had created a situation by making a decision to leave, thinking that it was going to be best for me and solve all my problems. Then the resolution to the messy situation was to go back to what I had left. There was no way to erase what I had done, but I will certainly spend the rest of my life enjoying what I have and appreciating the fact that I have worked hard my entire life to build my idea of the perfect life, and I am going to enjoy it. If I did not believe it before, I certainly do believe now that I am the luckiest woman on the planet. As cliché as it sounds, the saying, "The grass is greener where you water it," is so extremely true.

About the Author

Lisa D.A. Roberto is a wife, mother of three, and grandmother of two. She has always had a passion for books, initially as a way to escape and later as a way to experience. She started writing at an early age but did not let anyone read her stories. Opening up and making her stories public has been quite an experience for her. She appreciates the support and encouragement of her family and friends along this journey, and she is grateful to her readers for taking the time to read her stories.